# THE ANGEL SECRET

## DARK WORLD: THE ANGEL TRIALS 6

## MICHELLE MADOW

DREAMSCAPE PUBLISHING

# NOAH

$\mathcal{A}$s our rowboats made their way through Avalon, I looked around the island in wonder. I couldn't believe I was actually here. It had taken months, but I'd made it.

And the best thing in my life had happened to me along the way. Raven.

Before Raven, fate and destiny had always been something that happened to other people. Not to me.

Now I believed the quest the Earth Angel had sent me on had all been one grand plan so Raven and I would cross paths.

The journey had been long, but I wouldn't have had it any other way. And now Raven and I were finally here. Together. It felt unreal.

The boats entered a peaceful, winding cave, and I

was grateful not to be in the Vale anymore. So much horror had happened there. Avalon was a fresh start. A new beginning.

How many of my pack mates were also here on this island? I couldn't wait to find out. I'd always been a bit of a lone wolf, but I still needed my pack. All wolf shifters did. It was part of our nature.

I glanced back at Raven. She was sitting calmly in her boat behind mine. She smiled at me, and I could tell she was as elated to be at Avalon as I was.

Our rowboats pulled up to a dock, where Jacen was waiting. He wore black jeans and a black shirt. Casual, but still showing command. Two blonde women in big, bright, uncomfortable looking dresses stood next to him.

"Welcome to Avalon," Jacen said as our boats pulled up at the dock.

I stepped off the boat and onto the dock. Immediately, I went over to where Raven was getting out of her boat and held out a hand to help her out.

"Thanks," she said as she took my hand and stepped up onto the platform. Warmth rushed through my skin at her touch. She smiled shyly at me, like we were meeting for the first time.

I leaned in closer once she was beside me. She smelled

amazing—like citrus. The soap bars at the Haven complemented her natural scent nicely. "I wish we could have ridden in the same boat together," I murmured in her ear.

"Me too," she said. "Although I don't think the magic worked like that."

Of course, she was right. The magic needed us all in different rowboats, so we could all be taken to our own simulation.

"I saved you," I told her, unable to keep it to myself any longer. "When I was in that room and King Arthur was disguised as a doctor and made me choose between saving your life or the baby's life. I didn't need to think about it. I chose you."

"And I chose you," she said, although her eyes looked troubled. "Does that make us terrible people? That we saved each other instead of a baby prophesied to save the world?"

"No." I stared down at her, confident in my belief. "We're imprinted on each other. Someday—hopefully soon—we'll be mates. As my mate, you'll always be my priority, no matter what. And I'll be yours. Nothing is as precious to a shifter as his or her mate. If we wouldn't save each other no matter what, then we wouldn't have imprinted in the first place."

"But what about the baby?" she asked, still looking

troubled. "I can't even remember her name. I should, but I can't. What does that say about me?"

I flashed back to the scene in the simulation when King Arthur had given me the choice. He'd said the baby's name—I knew he had. But remembering it was like trying to grasp at water. I could touch it, but I couldn't hold onto it.

It was like the memory had been erased.

"I don't remember it either," I said. "I don't think we're meant to. And remember—the simulation wasn't real. You made it to Avalon because you're a good person. You're more than a good person. You're an *amazing* person. I know it, and now Avalon knows it, too."

"You're pretty amazing, too," she said.

"You know we all can hear you," Bella interrupted, glaring at us and crossing her arms. "Can the two of you tone down the love fest until you get yourselves a room?"

"Sorry." Raven's cheeks turned red. She put some more space between us, although she kept her hand in mine.

I didn't apologize. I'd never apologize for loving Raven. But Bella was right. In the time that Raven and I had been talking, the others had all gotten off their boats. So I turned my focus to Jacen and the women standing with him.

Until now, I'd been so focused on Raven that I hadn't paid attention to the women's scents. Now, I was blasted with the smell of them. It was like I was standing in a greenhouse full of flowers. The scent was similar to that of a light magic witch, but much stronger.

"What species are you?" I looked at the first woman, and then at the other. The first was wearing a red dress, and the other was wearing a purple dress. "I don't recognize your scent."

"Noah." Raven nudged me with her shoulder. "Don't be rude."

"Don't worry about it." The woman in red laughed. Her laugh was light and airy, like bells. "I'm Dahlia, and this is Violet. We're mages. And we're so thrilled to be here with Jacen to welcome you to Avalon."

## RAVEN

"You can't be mages," Bella said. "Mages don't exist."

"On the contrary," the woman in purple —Violet—said. "We're here, and I can assure you that we do indeed exist. There are three of us on Avalon, and our magic helps keep the island thriving."

"Where's the third?" Bella looked around, as if a third mage was going to pop out of a hidden corner of the cavern at any moment.

"Iris is planning the welcome feast for tonight," Dahlia said. "You'll meet her then. Violet and I always help Jacen orientate new arrivals to the island. It's such a pleasure to welcome you to our cause."

"And the Earth Angel?" I directed the question

toward Jacen, since the Earth Angel was his girlfriend. "I was hoping to meet her too."

That was the understatement of the century. I'd thought the Earth Angel would be with Jacen to greet us. But there was still no sight of her.

It was almost like she was purposefully avoiding meeting us.

If she were, I couldn't blame her. I was *not* happy with her after learning she'd used transformation potion to masquerade in my form and had my memories wiped against my will. I had no intention of pretending otherwise when we were finally face to face. I didn't care that she was one of the most powerful supernaturals in the world. What she did to me wasn't right.

She owed me an apology, at the least.

"The Earth Angel will also be at the banquet tonight," Jacen said. "You'll meet her there."

"We came all this way on a quest that *she* gave to Noah, and she can't bother greeting him on arrival?" Maybe I should have held back—after all, we were guests here—but I didn't. The Earth Angel not being here to welcome us was insulting.

"She's very busy." Jacen held my gaze, his silver eyes warning me to stop pushing the matter. "Managing an island of supernaturals is no easy task. But she's looking forward to greeting you tonight. Which is why she's holding an entire *banquet* to celebrate your arrival."

I couldn't argue against a banquet. So I pressed my lips together, figuring I'd pushed it enough for now. Jacen and I had had a pretty good rapport so far. No need to mess that up during my first five minutes on Avalon.

I'd meet the Earth Angel soon enough.

"That's very generous of her," Thomas finally spoke up from where he was standing at the edge of the group. He was holding his cell phone, the screen lit up like he'd just been using it.

"It is." Jacen nodded, looking pleased by Thomas's acknowledgment. Then he glanced at the phone in Thomas's hand. "There's no reception on Avalon," he said. "You'll find that phones are rather useless here."

"Not for me." Thomas smirked as his screen lit up again. "I texted Mary to let her know we arrived safely. She just replied and said she was glad to hear from me. She wishes us the best on Avalon, and asked me to reach out again if we need anything from the Haven."

"How...?" For the first time since I'd met him, Jacen looked thoroughly shocked.

"I'm a gifted vampire," Thomas said. "My gift is with technology. I've always had a knack for it."

"Apparently." Jacen eyed up Thomas's phone, looking

impressed. "Avalon hasn't been able to communicate with Earth through technology, and it's been a bit of a hassle for us to teleport back and forth to send and receive messages. Your gift will be highly useful to us here."

"Glad to help," Thomas said.

"Glad to have you here." Jacen nodded at him, then refocused on the rest of us. "As you can see, we're in a tunnel system underneath the island. The stairs behind me lead straight up to the castle. That's where all the main activity happens on Avalon. The mages have come with me to welcome you so they can bring you to the orientation rooms and start getting you adjusted to life here. The supernaturals will be following Dahlia, and Raven will follow Violet."

"No." Noah gripped my hand tighter and stepped closer to my side. "I go where Raven goes." He stared fiercely at Jacen, daring the vampire prince to contradict him.

Dahlia stepped forward, meeting Noah's eyes and giving him a small smile. "I'm afraid that's not possible," she said. "Supernaturals and humans have different orientation sessions to life on Avalon. This system has been in place since Avalon first opened up months ago. It exists to ensure your introductions to the island go as smoothly as possible."

"My introduction to the island will go as smoothly as possible if I remain by Raven's side." Noah narrowed his eyes in warning.

I held my gaze with Dahlia's as well, since I didn't want to leave Noah's side, either.

Why couldn't we all be "introduced to the island" together?

"You either come with me and the rest of the supernaturals, or you can leave." If Dahlia was affected by Noah's intense attitude, she didn't let it show. "Your choice."

"You and Raven will see each other at the banquet tonight," Violet chimed in. "Iris has incredible party planning skills. I'll make sure she knows to seat you and Raven next to each other."

All three of them—Dahlia, Violet, and Jacen— watched Noah and me expectantly. They clearly weren't budging. And we were newcomers to their island. Who were we to demand they changed the way things worked around here just because Noah and I hadn't left each other's sides since he'd rescued me from the bunker? We couldn't stay glued to each other forever.

I turned to Noah, resolved in my decision. "Avalon is the safest place on the planet," I said. "We've risked everything to be here. If humans and supernaturals have different orientation sessions, maybe there's a good reason for it."

"Good." Violet sighed. "At least one of you has sense."

Noah's eyes flicked back and forth between the mages and mine. *Are you sure?* he spoke to me through the imprint bond.

*I'm sure.* I gave his hand a small squeeze. *They're not budging, and we didn't work this hard to get here to turn back now.*

*I wasn't going to turn back.* He watched me so intensely that it was like he could see straight into my soul. *I was going to stand my ground until they gave in.*

He was so stubborn. I supposed we were similar in that way.

It was probably why we'd butted heads so much when we'd first met.

*We need to choose our battles carefully,* I said. *I'm sure the orientation sessions will be fine. And now we know I can communicate through the imprint bond through far distances. So if I need you before dinner, you'll be the first to know. I promise.*

Bella tapped her foot on the ground impatiently. "We all know you're talking to each other through the imprint bond," she said.

"Sorry." My cheeks heated, and I faced the mages again. I wanted to tell them that Noah would be doing as they'd asked, but that was his decision to make. Not mine.

"We can't stand here waiting forever," Dahlia said, her gaze pinned on Noah. "What'll it be?"

He continued staring her down, and my stomach flipped with panic that he was going to say no.

"I didn't work this hard to get here to turn back now," he finally said. "So please. Lead the way."

# NOAH

*A*s Jacen had said, the steps led up into the castle. Now we were in a grand hall, with plush rugs, carved wooden furniture, and colorful tapestries draped along the stone walls.

The mages fit right in, in their medieval styled dresses. The rest of us looked alien in the white cotton outfits we were wearing from the Haven.

"This is where we'll split ways," Dahlia said. "Raven, Violet will take you to your orientation. The rest of you, follow me."

I pulled Raven into a hug, my lips close to her ear. "Good luck," I said. "And remember, let me know if you need me."

"You know it." She smiled, looking radiant and confident that everything would be fine.

I wished I had that kind of optimism. But after everything I'd been through, I knew to keep my guard up everywhere.

Including Avalon.

"I'll see you at dinner," she said, pulling out of my embrace.

"Yeah," I said. "See you then."

"I'll see all of you all at dinner as well," Jacen said. "I have other business to attend to on Avalon until then. But you're in the best hands with Violet and Dahlia. They'll figure out what each of you can best contribute to the island. And tonight, we'll celebrate."

He zipped out of sight, leaving us alone with the mages.

Violet led Raven to the left, and Dahlia led the rest of us to the right. I didn't stop glancing at Raven over my shoulder until she turned the corner.

The moment she was out of sight, every muscle in my body tensed. All my instincts urged me to turn around and run back to her side, where I could protect her.

"Relax," Thomas said, glancing at me from the corner of his eye. "She'll be fine."

"I know."

"You sure about that?" he asked. "Because your racing pulse says otherwise."

I glared at him and made a conscious effort to breathe slowly to get my pulse back at a normal speed. I didn't say another word as we followed Dahlia to the end of the hall.

She opened a large wooden door, revealing a spiral stone staircase. "We'll be taking the stairs all the way to the top," she said. "And Thomas is right—you all need to relax. I'm taking you to orientation. Not to a prison cell." She lifted her skirts and made her way up the stairs.

The top ended up being the fifth floor. Dahlia opened the door and led us into a circular room inside the castle tower. There was a round table in the middle, set for five, with a covered silver platter and a pitcher of water in the center. Each wall had windows, giving us a stunning view of Avalon's luscious green mountains and bright blue lakes.

Dahlia clasped her hands in front of herself and smiled at each of us as we walked into the room. "Please, have a seat," she said, gesturing toward the table.

I claimed my seat—the one facing the door. If anyone came in during our orientation, I wanted to be the first to know.

Thomas took the seat next to me, also facing the door. I supposed he had the same idea. Jessica and Bella sat at both of our sides. The only seat remaining—Dahlia's—faced away from the door.

The blonde mage sat down, smoothed out her skirts, and smiled at us. "I imagine the four of you are hungry," she said. "People always are, after coming through the simulation and arriving at Avalon."

At the mention of food, my stomach rumbled. Audibly. A human might have missed it, but since everyone in the room had supernatural hearing, I knew they'd heard.

I could *really* go for a bacon cheeseburger right now. I doubted they had those on Avalon. But I could hope.

Dahlia reached forward and lifted the lid off the platter. Inside were strange white fruits I'd never seen before. There were enough pieces for a group more than twice our size. Each piece was perfectly round, and about the size of an orange.

And they had no smell.

*Everything* always had a smell. Especially fruit. But this white fruit in front of me smelled like nothing.

"Here you go," Dahlia said with a smile. "Dig in."

The mage must have lost her mind. Because this was *not* an actual meal.

"Fruit's what my food eats," I said. "Shifters need meat."

"Taste it," she said with a knowing smile. "I think you'll be surprised."

Thomas also looked suspicious. "Do you promise it's safe?" he asked. "Because it has no scent to it."

"The fruit's safe," she said. "Now, dig in. I know you're hungry." She glanced at me when she said that last part.

Cursed stomach betraying me by growling.

But no matter how hungry I was, I didn't trust her—or her strange fruit—that easily. Luckily, we had a walking lie detector with us.

I turned to Jessica. "Is she telling the truth?" I asked.

"Yes," Jessica said. "The fruit's safe."

"I'm guessing you're gifted as well?" Dahlia asked Jessica.

"I am." Jessica pressed her lips together and looked down at the table. "I can tell if people are lying or telling the truth."

"Why do you sound so unsure of yourself?" Dahlia asked.

"Because that was my gift as a human," Jessica said, meeting the mage's eyes again. "Apparently, our powers amplify once we're turned into vampires. But mine hasn't done that yet."

"Interesting," Dahlia said. "I'm sure we'll have it figured out for you soon enough." She gave Jessica an encouraging smile and focused again on the rest of us.

"Now, you heard the girl," she said. "The fruit's safe. So stop being so skeptical, and dig in."

I still didn't understand how she thought fruit was an entire meal. Maybe mages were all vegans or something. But it was all she was offering right now, and I was starving.

So I reached into the platter and plucked one of the strange white fruits out of it. It was smooth on the outside, like an apple. Not what I'd expected it to feel like. But oh well—nothing could be as bad as the meager squirrels I'd had to eat during a particularly rough winter in the Vale two years back.

"Here goes nothing," I said, lifting it to my mouth and taking a bite.

# NOAH

*a* bacon cheeseburger.

That's what the white fruit tasted like. It had the same texture as a bacon cheeseburger, and the same taste as a bacon cheeseburger. It was cooked exactly how I liked my meat—rare. It was even the perfect temperature.

I chewed and swallowed, looking at the fruit in amazement.

Dahlia was watching me, waiting anxiously for my reaction. So was everyone else at the table.

"Well?" Bella asked. "It looks like you liked it."

"It tastes like a bacon cheeseburger," I focused on Dahlia, resting an elbow on the table and holding the fruit up in front of me. "How's that possible?"

"I'll tell you soon," she said. "But first, the rest of you should try a piece, too."

Bella reached for the fruit and took a bite. Her eyes lit up as she chewed and swallowed. "Animal style fries from In N Out Burger," she said. "That's exactly what I was craving right now. My sisters and I eat *so* much In N Out Burger when we're stressed." She took another bite, looking just as amazed as I felt.

Thomas and Jessica were taking bites of the fruit, too. Thomas said his tasted like a rare rib eye, and Jessica said hers tasted like cookie dough ice cream.

I took another bite of mine, curious if the fruit changed taste with every bite. It was still bacon cheese-burger. Which I wasn't complaining about, because that was exactly what I wanted right now.

I finished the rest of the fruit in a few quick bites, and reached for another. It also tasted like a bacon cheeseburger. Incredible.

The only one of us who wasn't continuing to dig in was Thomas. He held the fruit a bit away from himself, like he didn't trust it. He looked at Dahlia like he didn't trust her, either.

"Why does the fruit taste different to each of us?" he asked.

"The fruit you're eating grows only on Avalon," she said. "It's called mana."

"Isn't that what Moses and his followers ate in the desert after escaping Egypt?" Jessica asked.

"That's manna, with two n's," Dahlia said. "It's similar to the mana that grows on Avalon. This mana grows in abundance from our trees, no matter the season. It tastes like whatever food you're craving at the moment. It can even taste like a food you've never tried before, if you're feeling adventurous. And the best part is that it contains every nutrient you need to keep your body running at peak performance. Eating mana is part of the reason why no one ages on Avalon."

"Hold up." That last part got me to stop chowing down on the delicious bacon cheeseburger. Mana. Whatever. "You mean this stuff makes us immortal?"

"It does." Dahlia nodded. "Everyone who comes to the island after the age of twenty-five stops aging while they're here. Those who come when they're younger will continue to age until they're twenty-five, and then their body will freeze in that state. If they venture off Avalon and start living on regular food again, they'll continue to age until returning to Avalon and eating the mana again."

"That's dangerous." Thomas's eyes darkened. "If anyone on Earth finds out about this, they'll go to a lot of trouble to get their hands on the mana and bring it to Earth."

"They might try," Dahlia said. "But they won't succeed. The mana disintegrates the moment it passes Avalon's boundary. Only those worthy to live on Avalon are able to eat it."

I nodded, still not fully processing the part about not aging if I continued eating this fruit. Shifters aged, as did witches and Nephilim. Vampires were the only supernaturals on Earth that were immortal.

I'd never thought immortality was a possibility for me until this moment. I wasn't sure if it was something I wanted or not.

It was too much to think about right now.

"What about Jessica?" I asked instead. "She's what… fifteen years old?"

"Sixteen." Jessica glared at me, like the year difference was massively offensive.

"Sixteen," I repeated. "Same difference. Will she age until she's twenty-five, now that she's on Avalon and eating mana? Or will she remain sixteen, since she's a vampire?"

"She'll remain sixteen," Dahlia said. "Vampires are frozen at the age they were when they were turned. Not even mana can change that."

"All right." Thomas still wasn't relaxed, although he didn't look as uptight as before, either. "So, mana tastes like whatever we want, and has every nutrient people need. But it didn't make me feel less thirsty. And as I'm sure you know, vampires need more than food to survive. We need blood, too."

Dahlia glanced at the silver pitcher next to the platter of mana. "Why don't you have some of that?" she asked.

"That's water," I said. "I can smell it from here."

"Water has a smell?" Bella's eyebrows knit in confusion.

"It's fresh and clean," I said. "It's hard to describe. But yes, it has a smell."

"Strange." She looked at me like I'd landed from another planet.

"Being able to smell water helps shifters survive in the outdoors," I explained. "And I promise you—that's water in the pitcher. Not blood."

"Try it," Dahlia repeated, motioning to the pitcher. "The water won't harm you. I promise."

Jessica reached for the pitcher, poured herself a glass of water, and took a sip.

Her eyes widened in amazement, and she quickly emptied the glass. Once done, she set it down on the table. "Oh my gosh," she said, looking to Thomas. "You have to try it."

"Why?" he asked.

"Just try it," she said, pouring some for him. "Trust me."

He gulped down all the water in his glass in a few seconds. "Incredible," he said once he was finished.

I reached for the pitcher and poured myself a glass, trying some of this special water for myself.

It tasted like normal water.

"I don't get it," I said, looking around at the others for answers. "What's so special about this water?"

# NOAH

"*B*efore drinking it, I was thirsty," Thomas said darkly. "For *blood*. But somehow, that water took away my thirst. Which shouldn't be possible. The only thing that should be able to do that is actual blood." He turned his focus to Dahlia. "What did you put in the water?" he asked.

"I didn't put anything in the water," she said. "The water in that pitcher is Holy Water. *All* fresh water on Avalon is Holy Water."

"The water that angels have to dip weapons into to turn them into Holy Weapons," I said, brushing my fingers against my slicer in my weapons belt.

"Exactly." Dahlia nodded. "When consumed by vampires, Holy Water refreshes them just like human blood. Therefore, vampires on Avalon don't need blood. Everyone here can survive on mana and Holy Water alone. Although, we do serve alcohol on special occasions. Because what fun is life without a bit of wine?" She laughed, clearly amusing herself.

How could a person be so perky?

"I'm more of a beer guy myself," I said casually.

"We have that, too." She smiled, not picking up on how annoying I found her overly perky attitude to be. Or she didn't care.

"Back to the subject of Holy Water," Thomas said, always the one to stay focused. "How much of it is on Avalon?"

"It's endless," Dahlia said. "Avalon supplies what its citizens need. Everyone here is well taken care of. I promise you that."

"I'm glad to hear it." He leaned forward, looking like the gears in his brain were working on overdrive. "Because we need to export it to vampires around the world."

Dahlia frowned, suddenly somber. "Jacen said the same thing at first," she said. "But he discovered that just like mana, Holy Water loses its magic once it's brought past the boundary. Both mana and Holy Water must be consumed on Avalon to be effective."

Thomas deflated, Dahlia's words taking the hope

straight out of him. He was back to the steel hard, down to business Thomas we all knew and loved. Well, tolerated.

"Now that you have food and water, it's time to continue with the orientation," Dahlia said. "It's my job to assign all new supernaturals positions on Avalon. We'll start with each of you telling me your strengths and weaknesses."

"What is this?" Bella chuckled. "Circle time?"

"What's circle time?" I asked.

"Something we had to do at school when we were kids," she said simply.

"Right." I nodded, still having no clue what she was talking about. Growing up in the wild, I'd never had school in the traditional sense that the supernaturals living alongside the human community had experienced. We learned about the land and how to survive in it and contribute to the pack from the elders. But we did gather in circles to tell stories, which might have been similar to this "circle time" Bella was talking about.

"Who wants to start?" Dahlia looked around our group, waiting for someone to begin.

I plucked another piece of mana from the platter and took a large bite. Someone else could share his or her strengths and weaknesses first. I wanted to eat.

"I guess I'll start," Jessica said timidly.

"Wonderful." Dahlia brought her hands together and beamed. "Why don't you start with your greatest strength?"

"My greatest strength is my gift of telling lies from truths," Jessica said quickly. "But my gift is also my weakness, since I don't know how it's grown since I've turned into a vampire. I was only turned a few days ago. I can't fight or use my heightened senses like Thomas can. It's all a blur of new information, and it's confusing. I think I only got through the simulation we had to pass to get here because of sheer luck."

"No one gets to Avalon because of luck," Dahlia said. "If you didn't deserve to be here, then you wouldn't be here. Simple as that. There are reasons for everything that happens in life. We might not know what those reasons are yet, but it doesn't make them less real."

Jessica nodded, which I guessed meant Dahlia was telling the truth. Or at least the truth as she believed it. Which led to an interesting question...

"How exactly does your gift work?" I asked Jessica. "For instance, let's say someone *thinks* something is the truth, but what they think is the truth is wrong. Would you be able to tell that the truth they believe to be true is incorrect?"

I hoped I'd explained that properly. Because it put me in circles thinking about it.

"I can only tell if someone is telling the truth as they believe it," she said. "For example, let's say two people of different religious beliefs were telling me about their faith. Both of what they were saying would register as true, because *they* believed it. My gift can't tell me what's true or not in the world. It simply tells me if someone is being honest with me—as they know it—or if they're lying."

"Interesting," I said. "Thanks for clearing that up."

"Yes," Dahlia chimed in. "It certainly is very interesting."

Dahlia just couldn't handle not leading a conversation, could she?

"And don't worry—there's a place for you in Avalon," she assured Jessica. "But I'm going to listen to everyone's strengths and weaknesses before making those places official. So... Bella. How about you go next?"

"That's easy," Bella said. "My strength is dark magic —both potions and spells. My weakness is close combat."

"You did a great job fighting those demons in the bunker," I pointed out.

"We were invisible," she said. "It made it easier. I mean, I'm not terrible at close combat—if I were, I wouldn't have been a good choice to join you on that mission—but it's definitely a weak spot of mine. When it comes to fighting, I prefer doing it from a distance. Like when I shot those potion bombs at Abaddon's Locust in the field."

I remembered the moment well. She'd shot complacent potion at the Locust to give Thomas and me an advantage over the monster.

I also guessed she didn't mention the type of potion bomb on purpose. Complacent potion was illegal. Any witch found creating it would be brought to the Haven, where she'd have a trial that would end up in her magic being stripped.

"Thanks for sharing," Dahlia said, turning her focus to Thomas and me. "Which one of you wants to go next?"

I took another huge bite of the mana and chewed, staring at Thomas in challenge.

I wasn't sure why I wanted to go last.

Maybe I wanted to hear everyone else's weaknesses before I admitted mine.

"Since Noah is lacking table manners, I suppose I'm up next," Thomas said, which only prompted me to make my next bite of mana even larger. He cleared his throat, and continued, "My strength is my gift with technology. And my weakness is luxury cars."

Dahlia's eyes flashed with confusion.

I had to stop myself from laughing, since my mouth was full of mana.

"I take it you're joking?" Dahlia asked.

"No." Thomas straightened his cuffs and sat back. "I truly have a weakness for luxury cars. You should see my garage at the Bettencourt."

"You should," I agreed, now that I'd finished chewing. "It's pretty impressive."

"Was that a compliment?" Thomas stared at me in pretend shock.

"Don't get too excited," I joked. "I was complimenting the cars. Not you."

He smirked, and I couldn't help returning the look. Mainly because Dahlia's irritated expression made her appear slightly constipated. And I could tell we were both amused by it.

If someone had told me weeks ago that Thomas Bettencourt was going to grow on me, I'd never believe them. *I* still didn't quite believe it.

Strange things happened when you were forced to work with your enemies to help save the world.

"Seriously," Dahlia said. "What's your real weakness?"

Thomas glanced out the window across from him, his eyes going dark and distant. It was like he was no longer in the room with us.

Everyone stopped moving and eating. Silence descended upon the room like a wet blanket.

"Sage Montgomery," Thomas finally said. "She's my weakness. She's been my weakness since the moment I met her, and she'll be my weakness for the rest of my immortal existence."

## NOAH

"Who's Sage Montgomery?" Dahlia asked.

"Sage is the love of my life, and the shifter I've imprinted on," Thomas said. "She and her pack have been blood bound with the greater demon Azazel. To break the bond, Azazel needs to be killed. I'd do it myself, but we all know that only the Nephilim can kill Azazel. That's why I came to Avalon. To work with the Nephilim and rescue Sage."

Dahlia's breathing grew shallow as Thomas spoke. She looked around the room like a bird trapped in a cage, refusing to look at Thomas. A rusty scent rose from her skin. Anxiety.

"You're anxious," I said to her. "Why?"

The scent amplified when I spoke. But she turned to me and smiled, her face a mask of calm. Anyone without supernatural shifter senses wouldn't have been able to tell how worried she was.

"The blood binding spell you speak of is an ancient spell," she said quickly. "The knowledge of how to cast it was supposedly destroyed with the witch circle that created it. If Thomas is correct and the spell is being used again... we're in for a harder fight than anticipated."

"Of course I'm correct," Thomas said. "After the blood binding spell was completed, I saw Sage myself. She wasn't Sage anymore. She was a shell of who she used to be. If even."

"This is grave news." Dahlia lowered her head in respect, refusing to look at any of us. "I'll send word to the Earth Angel once we finish up here. Thank you for sharing, Thomas." She paused to collect herself. "Now, we have one more left." She faced me, worry still in her eyes. "Your turn, Noah."

"My strength is close combat in my wolf form," I said. "Although I'm skilled with swords and knives in my human form as well. And my weakness..." I looked down at my empty plate, embarrassed at what I was about to say. But everyone else had admitted their weaknesses. I could do it too.

So I pulled myself together and forced myself to meet Dahlia's eyes.

"I don't know how to read or write," I said. "The packs in the Vale were at war constantly, each pack fighting for control over the best land. So we were always moving around. I know how to hunt, how to live off the land, how to find shelter, and how to fight. But reading and writing weren't necessary to survive in the Vale. So I never learned. All of our history, stories, and knowledge were passed down orally through the elders."

"Thank you for sharing," Dahlia said with a polite nod. "I can tell that wasn't easy for you. But you'll be happy to know that members of the Vale packs are here at Avalon. They also came to us unable to read and write, and we've been successful in teaching them. I'm sure you'll pick up on it just as easily."

"You're going to teach me?" I asked, stunned.

"Of course." She raised her chin, as if anything else was unacceptable. "Well, not myself specifically. But we have teachers here for that. You'll be learning how to read and write for half of your day, and training shifter students for the other half of the day."

"Training them in what?" I asked.

"Fighting, of course," she said. "The wolves from the Vale are skilled in combat, which makes sense, given the volatile history of the area. But there are also shifters who have come to us from more urban environments. Not many, mind you—most shifters tend to prefer living in the great outdoors—but there are some. They need a good teacher. And if rumor proves true, you're one of the best fighters around. Especially when it comes to fighting demons."

"I killed ten demons and brought their teeth here to prove it," I said. "So yeah, I'm not so bad at it."

"As I thought," she said, continuing on to focus on the others. "Bella, you'll be working with the Avalon witches on creating potions and casting spells. Thomas will be the leader of our new technology team, which will be responsible for creating and maintaining internet connectivity throughout the island and with Earth, along with any other technological help that will benefit Avalon. Jessica will be a student at Avalon Academy, and will be introduced to life as a vampire and taught how to fight. I'll send word to your superiors about your assignments. Does anyone have any questions?"

"I do," I said, and all eyes turned to me. "You said I'll be training shifters. But while Raven and I were on the road, I started training her. I want to continue training her to prepare her for the Angel Trials."

"Absolutely not," Dahlia said. "There are strict requirements to train for the Angel Trials. Our head trainers at the academy have it covered. Raven is in the best of hands with them."

I sat back, annoyed. Because on one hand, I understood what Dahlia was saying. Raven needed the best training possible to get through the Angel Trials. Seeing as I knew nothing about the Trials, I understood why I wouldn't be top pick for the job.

But I loved Raven. No other trainer would care as much about her progress as I did.

So I was going to help her prepare for what was ahead, whether Dahlia liked it or not.

# RAVEN

*I* sat with Violet at a small table on the top floor of one of the castle turrets. The circular room made me feel like Rapunzel in her tower. And the view out of all the windows—the green mountains, the crystal blue ocean—left me breathless.

I couldn't believe I was finally at Avalon.

Violet told me that the room we were in was identical to the one in the other tower, where Noah and the others were going through their orientation with Dahlia. The mage was soft spoken and kind as she explained the mana and Holy Water to me.

"It will really taste like whatever I want?" I asked.

"It will." She nodded, excited. Her eyes were the same color as her name. "Try it."

I reached into the platter to take a piece of the

strange white fruit. It fit perfectly in my hand. But it was weird looking. Was it truly safe to eat?

Jacen had sent us to orientation with the mages, and I trusted Jacen. So I pushed the doubt from my mind and took a tentative bite of the fruit.

It tasted like a perfectly cheesy burrito. The best burrito I'd ever had in my life. I felt my eyes light up the moment I tasted it.

I was so hungry that I felt like I could eat all the pieces of mana on the platter. And then some.

"And this is actually good for me?" I asked once I'd finished chewing. "Even though it tastes like a burrito?"

"The mana will give your body all the nutrients it needs to function at its best possible level," Violet said. "You'll feel stronger than ever."

"How's that possible?"

"Magic." She smiled. "We have a lot of that here on Avalon. As you learned earlier, my sisters and I are mages. Mages specialize in plant magic, or any magic connected to nature. Our presence here keeps the mana growing and the Holy Water flowing."

I took another bite of mana, chewing thoughtfully. I had a lot of questions. But Violet was fascinating, and since I was sitting here alone with her, the best place to start felt like asking her about herself.

"What exactly is a mage?" I asked. "I'm relatively

new to the supernatural world—I didn't know it existed until recently. Noah filled me in on a lot when I joined his demon hunt, but he never mentioned mages."

"He never mentioned us because there's no record of us ever living on Earth. Only rumors that have turned into myths," she said kindly. "You see, mages come from another realm. Mystica."

"Is Mystica similar to Avalon?" I hadn't been aware that other realms even existed until coming to Avalon. The entire time I'd been with Noah on his hunt, I'd assumed Avalon was a hidden place on Earth. Learning it was a different realm had been a shock in itself.

Now learning that there were *more* realms? It was a lot to take in.

"Not exactly," she said. "Avalon is unique, because it's a blessed island anchored to Earth. Avalon was created by the angels back when King Arthur passed away, as a resting place for him and a place for future Nephilim to live in safety. Mystica, on the other hand, is a world in itself. There are many different worlds, all of them parallel to Earth, and none of them touching each other. There's only one common link between the worlds. The Tree of Life."

"The actual Tree of Life?" This was getting crazier by the second. I placed the mana down, unable to focus on eating. "You mean the one from the Bible—the one Eve ate the apple from?"

"That's the Tree of Knowledge," Violet explained. "It's another powerful tree, but completely different from the Tree of Life. The Tree of Life is also referred to as the World Tree. It connects all the different worlds to each other."

"How many worlds are there?" I asked.

"Many," she said with a patient smile—a smile that also said she wasn't going to give me a specific number. "Earth, and Mystica, and most of all the other worlds are like leaves on the branches of the Tree. Then there are Heaven and Hell—which we compare to the sky and the ground. Heaven is above all the worlds, and Hell is below them. The angels watch over us all, and the demons linger below the surface.

"Thousands of years ago, humans stumbled upon the Tree of Life on Earth," she continued. "They started venturing into other worlds—Mystica included. The humans were safe in Mystica, as mages love and protect all living creatures. But many of the other realms weren't as kind to them. So the mages took action. We rescued as many of the humans from other realms as possible and brought them to Mystica. Once we'd saved as many as possible, we erased their memories of the Tree of Life and of all the realms beyond it before sending them back to Earth. Once they were safely returned, we cast spells around the Tree of Life to prevent humans from stumbling upon it again. But there was a small catch. You see, while humans were in Mystica, some of them became intimate with the mages. Many women became pregnant during that time. Months later, on Earth, they gave birth to the first of what you all call witches."

"So all witches are descendants of mages," I repeated, making sure I was getting this straight.

"Yes." Violet nodded. "Mages have similar powers as witches, but much stronger. Our magic is within us. Using it comes as naturally to us as breathing. We don't need spells or potions to use our magic—we can simply *use* it. Naturally, the first witches were much less powerful than mages, as they were half human. Witch magic has continued to get diluted from generation to generation. That's why the strongest witch circles are insistent about reproducing only with other witches. As I hear, it's become somewhat of a controversy amongst the witch circles here on Earth."

"I don't know." I shrugged, since Noah and Sage hadn't told me much about that. They'd told me mainly about shifters, and a decent amount about vampires. But it seemed like witches were an enigma even to them. "But I do know that female witches are the powerful ones, and male witches have little to no power. Is that true for the mages as well?"

"Females and males are both equally capable of magic in Mystica," Violet said. "My sisters and I only recently learned about male witches lacking power on Earth. We believe it has something to do with the way human chromosomes carry magic. As we've learned it, women have two X chromosomes, whereas men have an X and a Y chromosome. Our guesses are that either humans need two X chromosomes to fully perform magic, or that the Y chromosome inhibits the use of magic. We can't say for sure. Especially since magic oftentimes defies science. Both magic and science are valid, of course, but they tend to exist on different planes entirely. Sometimes they connect, but oftentimes they don't."

"Okay," I said, my mind racing as I took this all in. "But what about the female mages that got pregnant by human men? Wouldn't they have given birth to witches in Mystica?"

"Mystica is a lovely realm, but it's strict," Violet said. "It's remained one of the safest realms in the universe because mages have strong magic. We were scared of mixed raced children—witches—lessening our magic. So all mage women who got pregnant with half human babies were forced to give up their children."

My eyes widened in horror. "You mean their children were murdered?"

"No!" Violet gasped, repulsed at the suggestion. "Mages value all life. We would never do such a thing. The half human children—the witches—were taken to Earth and placed into the care of loving families. It was ensured that the families they were given to lived near human women who had given birth to half mage children. That way, they could be around others like themselves. And that, we believe, is how the original witch circles were formed."

"The mage women were okay with giving their children up like that?"

"I doubt it." Violet's eyes hardened. "No one knows for certain how it was handled. Our history books say our women were happy to send their children to Earth, as Earth was the best place for them to grow up. I'm not sure how much I believe it. Dahlia does, but I question it. You see, I've yet to become a mother myself, but I'd never give a child of mine up without a fight. All I know is that none of the witch children remained in Mystica."

I nodded, agreeing with Violet that it likely didn't go down as easily as their mage historians claimed. "You said the mages casted spells around the Tree of Life to hide it once the humans were returned to Earth," I said.

"So how did they drop the witch children off from Mystica?"

"We didn't hide the Tree of Life from ourselves," she said. "We could come and go as we pleased. Although we've chosen to stay in Mystica until recently."

"What happened recently?" I asked.

"When my sisters and I were born, a faerie ventured into our realm," she said. "Prince Devyn—the only fae in existence who's ever had the power of omniscient sight. It was a rare occurrence, as the fae prefer to stay in their realm, the Otherworld. Prince Devyn told our parents that we were reaching a crucial point in the timeline of the universe—a point that would determine whether the universe took a sharp turn toward either the dark or the light. He gave them instructions. He said that once my sisters and I reached fourteen years old, we were to go to Earth and live in a house on the shores of Norway. There, we were to wait for the arrival of the last Nephilim on Earth and guide her toward the Tree of Life, because only mages could help someone from Earth get past the spells our ancestors had cast around the Tree that hid it from them." She paused to take a sip of water, and then continued, "After getting the message to our parents, Prince Devyn returned to the Other-world, telling them nothing more. But our parents knew the birth of triplets was a sign. In Mystica, it's hard enough to get pregnant with one child, let alone three. So they trusted Prince Devyn. They raised my sisters and I with full awareness of our destiny. And so, on our fourteenth birthday, we stepped into the Tree and entered Earth, easily finding the house Prince Devyn had told our parents about. We lived there in solitude for five years."

"That must have been lonely," I said.

"It was." Her violet eyes went distant for a moment, but she refocused a second later. "But we made a home for ourselves there. We even became acquainted with some of the humans around town, although we made sure to never get *too* close. Prince Devyn had warned us that getting too close to anyone on Earth could severely alter the course of the future. Plus, we always knew that Earth wasn't our true home. So we waited in that house until a few months ago, when the prophesied Nephilim finally arrived. Annika, who would soon become the Earth Angel."

# RAVEN

"So you knew Annika before she was the Earth Angel." I knew Annika hadn't always been an Earth Angel—she'd been human first, and then Nephilim. Noah had told me as much during our road trip. But the story of how she'd become the Earth Angel had always been vague. I suspected because Noah didn't know all of it himself.

"I did." Violet nodded. "My sisters and I directed her toward the Tree of Life. She gained entrance into the Tree and went all the way to Heaven. There, she drank from the Grail and became the Earth Angel."

"But you didn't go home to Mystica after helping her," I said. "You stayed here. Why?"

"Avalon is our forever home," she said. "My sisters and I supply magic to the island to allow it to thrive.

47

Staying here has always been our destiny. Especially because if the demons win the war here on Earth, they could gain access to the Tree of Life. Then they could enter the other realms—including Mystica. By helping the Earth Angel and her army, we're not just protecting Earth, but *all* the realms in the universe."

"It sounds like the creatures living in the other universes should be coming here to help us, too," I said.

"They won't," Violet said simply. "Most of the other realms are so involved with their own problems that Earth isn't on their radar. And the demons are only threatening Earth right now. It's remarkably easy for an entire society—or realm—to ignore a problem until it directly affects them. So I doubt they'll help Earth until the demons start trying to invade their worlds. *If* it gets to that point. Hopefully it never will."

"Because we'll beat the demons first," I said.

"That's the goal," Violet said. "And it's why you came here. To go through the Angel Trials, become a Nephilim, and join the Earth Angel's army. Correct?"

"It is," I said. "Speaking of, what should I expect from the Angel Trials?" I sat straighter, ready to learn. All I'd heard until now was that the Angel Trials were going to be challenging. No one outside of Avalon knew more than that.

Now that I was here, I was ready to find out what I'd be doing to become a Nephilim.

After surviving Noah's demon hunt, there was no challenge I couldn't handle. Maybe it was the mana and Holy Water, or maybe it was because I'd finally made it to Avalon, but I felt ready to take on the world.

"Raven." Violet said my name as if she were bracing me for something. "There's something important you need to know about the Angel Trials."

"Yes?" Unease rolled through my stomach. Because the way she was looking at me wasn't good.

"There are many steps—or as we call them, trials—to becoming a Nephilim," she said. "First, the human must make it through King Arthur's simulation to get to Avalon. You completed that part, which isn't easy."

"Thanks." I smiled, recalling the simulation and King Arthur. It was still crazy to believe I'd met the legendary king himself.

"Next, the body must be strengthened so it's ready to drink angelic blood from the Holy Grail," she said. "The Grail turns human blood into Nephilim blood, although their powers will be latent."

"So drinking from the Grail doesn't turn a human into a Nephilim?"

"The transition isn't complete at that point," she said. "To ignite Nephilim powers, a person with Nephilim blood needs to kill a supernatural. We've arranged a safe environment for this to happen, where the supernatural being killed is one that has committed grave crimes and has already been sentenced to death. If they're going to die, it might as well help our cause. But no one has yet to make it to that point."

"Why not?" I fiddled with my hands under the table. She was going to say something I didn't want to hear—I knew it.

I wished she'd get it over with already.

"Many have passed the first two steps," she said. "Getting to Avalon and completing the strength training. But when it comes to drinking from the Grail, we've encountered a problem."

"What kind of a problem?" It was clear by now that Violet needed to be prodded. She wasn't enjoying telling me this any more than I was enjoying waiting for her to drop whatever bomb was coming.

"No one has yet to drink from the Grail and survive," she said. "They've all rejected the angel blood and died on the spot."

# RAVEN

"*W*hat?" I wasn't sure what I'd expected her to say. It certainly hadn't been that.

"No one has survived drinking—"

"I heard you the first time," I cut her off, since I hadn't misheard. I just couldn't believe it was true. I didn't *want* to believe it was true. "Do you mean there are no Nephilim on Avalon?"

"Correct." She lowered her eyes, ashamed. "There are also no humans on Avalon. At least, not anymore."

"What do you mean?" I sat back in shock. Had the supernaturals on Earth been playing a giant joke on me by encouraging me to go to Avalon? It didn't make any sense.

"At first, we assumed the first few humans who drank from the Grail simply weren't strong enough to survive the transition." She spoke softly, remarkably calm despite what she was saying. "All of our history books say the strength training we gave them should have been sufficient, but we tried training them harder anyway. It didn't work. They continued to die. Eventually, humans decided to leave Avalon instead of continuing on to what appeared to be a death sentence. They had their memories wiped, of course—we couldn't risk anyone from the outside world finding out what was going on here. A few of the strongest, most determined humans remained, convinced they'd be the ones to break the cycle. But they all died. Now there are no more left." She shrugged, looking just as defeated as those humans must have felt.

"No." I shook my head, horrified. The world spun out of control around me, and I had to hold onto the edge of the table to stay steady. I could barely breathe, or even think.

Everything I'd been hoping for since meeting Rosella at the Pier was crushed. Saving my mom, saving humanity... I couldn't do all of that if I didn't go through the Angel Trials and become a Nephilim.

"This can't be true." If I repeated it enough, maybe I'd believe it.

"I'm not lying to you," Violet said. "I'm telling you

this so you can make an informed decision about how you want to move forward."

"What do you mean?" I forced myself to focus, despite the doomsday scenarios racing through my mind. "What are my options?"

"You can either stay here or return home," she said. "This decision is why we have separate orientations for the supernaturals and the humans. It's our responsibility to let all humans who come to Avalon know what happened to those before them, so you can understand what you're facing. The Earth Angel has insisted upon it."

"Everyone on Earth believes the Earth Angel is turning humans into Nephilim to create an army that will be able to defeat the greater demons," I said, angry now. "They're counting on her. But it's all a lie."

"It's not a lie," Violet said. "The Earth Angel is working on a solution. Once she finds it, she'll resume building her army. But she needs time."

"Where's the Earth Angel?" I set my hands down flat upon the table, furious that the Earth Angel had sent Violet to deliver this news to me instead of telling me herself. "Everyone keeps talking to me about her, but I've never even seen her. I want to speak with her."

"It's not time for you to meet the Earth Angel yet," Violet said.

"Then when will I be meeting her?"

"Tonight at the banquet. The Earth Angel will be overseeing the feast. You and the others will meet her then."

"I don't think you understand." I stared straight at her, making sure she took me seriously. "I want to speak with the Earth Angel in *private*. Before the banquet."

"I'm afraid that's not possible," she said. "The Earth Angel is extremely busy running Avalon. My sisters and I speak for her."

"You've got to be kidding me." I huffed, feeling like we were getting nowhere.

"I'm completely serious." Violet's expression remained the same.

"It's a saying." I shook my head and squeezed the bridge of my nose with my fingers. Then I dropped my hand back down to my side and continued, "I know you're serious. But within the past few months, the Earth Angel had me abducted, kept me in a dungeon to use my blood for transformation potion, masqueraded around in my form while pretending to be 'Princess Ana of the Seventh Kingdom,' and then wiped my memory before sending me home. Maybe she thinks I don't remember. But I know what she did. And after all of that, the least she can give me is a few precious seconds of her time."

"I know you've been through a lot," Violet said, somehow still remaining calm. "But you have to understand how busy the Earth Angel is—"

"No," I interrupted her. "I don't think you do understand what I've been through. I knew for *months* that my memories had been tampered with. Then my mom was abducted by the greater demon Azazel from *our own home.* Then a psychic told me that to save her, I had to come to Avalon to become a Nephilim. I almost died trying to get here. Now I've finally made it, and not only do I find out that everyone who's tried to become a Nephilim has *died*, but the Earth Angel won't even speak with me? It's not acceptable. So I need you to tell her that I'm here, and that I insist on speaking with her. Now." I narrowed my eyes and continued staring at her, daring her to contradict me.

If Mary and Noah were right about my gift being my stubbornness and determination, it was time for my gift to work.

"I see you're not going to let this go." Violet stood up and walked over to a side table. She opened a drawer, pulling out a piece of parchment and a fancy pen. Then she sat back down and started writing, the pen flying across the parchment.

"What are you doing?" I asked.

"Writing a message to the Earth Angel on your

behalf." She didn't look up at me as she continued to write. "Unless you've changed your mind about wanting to speak with her?" She smiled, and I relaxed slightly at her attempt at humor.

"No." I sat back, amazed that it had worked. "Keep writing."

She finished up the letter by signing her name with a flourish at the bottom. Then she folded it and held it up in the air. She stared at it, and purple flames burst from her palm, the blazing fire surrounding the parchment.

The flames died down, and the letter was gone.

"Why did you do that?" I stared in shock at her empty palm.

"To plead your case to the Earth Angel." She looked at me like my question was stupid. Then, realization dawned on her soft features. "Right," she said. "You've never seen a fire message."

"No," I said. "I haven't."

"Fire messages are how mages and high powered witches send messages to each other," she said. "On Earth, they've mostly been replaced with texts and phone calls. But they come in handy on Avalon, where technology doesn't work."

"So you just sent that message to the Earth Angel," I said, and she nodded. "But you said only mages and high powered witches can send fire messages. How will she reply?"

"The Earth Angel will get a reply to us," she said. "Be patient."

We sat there waiting for a few minutes. Violet munched on a piece of mana, making no effort to chat. She seemed nervous. So it was up to me to keep the conversation going. Which wasn't hard, since I had a lot of questions.

"What are Noah and the others doing?" I asked.

"They're in a similar room, getting placed into jobs on Avalon by Dahlia."

"Is she going to tell them about the Angel Trials?" I asked. "About no human has yet to pass them?"

"She will," Violet said. "At the end of their orientation."

I wondered how Noah would react. He'd probably freak out, just like I was doing now.

How had so many months gone by with no humans passing the Angel Trials? And why was the Earth Angel allowing the supernaturals on Earth to believe she was successfully turning humans into Nephilim?

It was so messed up. My grievances against the Earth Angel had just increased tenfold. She had a *lot* to answer to, and I had no idea how she could possibly explain herself.

I also had no idea what I was going to do after speaking to her. Because if the Angel Trials were killing everyone who entered them... what was going to happen to me?

It was terrifying to think about. Which why I had to take this one step at a time. First, I needed to speak with the Earth Angel. Then I'd figure out what to do moving forward. Because I wouldn't give up. Not on my mom... and not on the world.

A knock on the door tore me from my thoughts.

"Come in." Violet sat straighter and ran her fingers through her dark hair.

A tall woman with long brown hair let herself in. She wore a floor-length black dress, and her stomach protruded slightly, as if she were pregnant. Or she could have just had a really big meal. It was that confusing point where it would be rude to ask when the baby was due because it might insult her.

"Camelia." Violet nodded at the woman, who nodded at her in return. "What brings you all the way up here?"

"A message from the Earth Angel." She focused on me, her gaze pointed and hard. There was something off about her eyes. Something sinister. "She wants me to bring Raven Danvers to her quarters at once."

*C*amelia didn't bother talking to me as she led me through the airy halls of the castle. She didn't even turn to look at me. If I wasn't hurrying to keep up, I was pretty sure she wouldn't notice altogether.

I didn't bother making small talk with her. She clearly wasn't in the mood for it. I wasn't, either.

I was too focused on the butterflies in my stomach at the thought of finally coming face to face with the Earth Angel. Sure, I'd put on a confident act back there with Violet. But I was ridiculously anxious. I mean, this was the *Earth Angel*. One of the most powerful beings in the world.

And I was about to face her down and tell her how angry I was with her.

Hopefully she didn't incinerate me on the spot.

She wouldn't do that, right? Angels were on the *good* side. They wouldn't incinerate people for speaking their minds. Especially when the person in question—AKA me—was correct.

I was so lost in my thoughts that I was barely paying attention to where we were walking. I knew we took a bunch of stairs and walked down a bunch of halls. Big, castle-like halls that looked like they came straight out of a medieval romance story. I was only brought back to the present when Camelia stopped in front of a grand double door entrance, the wood engraved with delicate flowers and vines. Luckily, I stopped a second before walking into her.

I doubted the frosty woman would take kindly to me stepping on her shoes.

Camelia pressed a hand against one of the doors and pushed it open. "Earth Angel," she said, "May I present Raven Danvers."

I took that as my cue, and entered the room.

It was big and grand, with hardwood floors, a woven rug, a majestic chandelier, and a king-sized canopy bed. Reclining on the bed was a dark haired, pale girl who looked younger than me.

She was an absolute mess.

Her hair was greasy—like she hadn't showered in

days—and was pulled up into a messy bun on the top of her head. Her legs were under the covers, and she was wearing an oversized sweatshirt that said *Panic! At the Disco* on it. Her face was drawn, like she hadn't been eating enough. And there were puffy, dark circles under her eyes, like she hadn't slept in weeks.

But her eyes... they were gold. Not brown with a little hint of yellow, but *gold*. I'd never seen eyes like that before. They were downright inhuman. And somehow, despite how frail she looked, there was a glow about her that made her beautiful. Like she was surrounded by an aura of golden warmth.

"Earth Angel?" I asked, question in my tone.

"Raven Danvers." She shot me a small smile, her voice light and kind. "It's so nice to meet you."

I stood there dumbfounded, unable to believe she was truly the Earth Angel. I guess I'd expected big fluffy wings, a white gown, a halo—the works. But this girl in front of me looked like a college student in bed with the flu. Not a powerful being in charge of a magical, mystical island.

Still, it didn't change everything she'd done to me.

"This isn't the first time we met." I clenched my fists as anger fueled my veins. She might look fragile and innocent, but she wasn't. "You remember that time. But

I don't. Because you took my memories from me. I told you not to, but you did it anyway."

She arched a brow. If I'd shocked her, she was certainly good at playing it cool. Then she turned to the intimidating woman who had led me into her chambers. "Camelia," she said. "You can leave us alone now."

Camelia did as asked, shutting the huge doors behind her.

Once she was gone, I turned back to the Earth Angel. Her golden eyes watched me with a mix of suspicion and curiosity.

"How do you know about your erased memories?" she asked.

"I've known something was off in my memories since returning home in January." I stood straighter, finding it easy to stay strong when the Earth Angel looked so weak. "Then, when I arrived at the Haven after helping Noah complete his quest, Mary told me everything."

"Why would Mary do that?" she asked.

"I pretended I remembered more than I did." I shrugged. "It was enough to get her to admit to enough that she had to come fully clean."

"So... you tricked the vampire queen of the Haven?"

If I didn't know better, I'd say the Earth Angel sounded impressed.

"I guess." I couldn't help but smirk. "I suppose it was part of my gift."

"Your gift?" The Earth Angel tilted her head, like a curious bird.

I was starting to wonder if she was capable of speaking more than a few parroted words back at me at a time.

"I take it you know about gifted humans?" I didn't bother hiding my irritation. We weren't going to get anywhere if the Earth Angel kept faking dumb. And I assumed she was pretending, since there was no way she could become the Earth Angel if she was truly clueless.

"Of course I do." She smiled a bit, as if she could read my mind.

Maybe she *could* read my mind? I didn't know what powers she had.

So I quickly thought of something ridiculous—the way my grandma's cat twitched and gave a serious side eye whenever someone tried taking her favorite stuffed toy from her. The Earth Angel didn't crack a smile.

Good—she couldn't read minds.

"What's your gift?" she pressed.

"Stubbornness," I said, crossing my arms over my chest. "I like getting my way."

That elicited the first true smile from her since I'd arrived in her chambers. "That's the least surprising thing I've heard all day," she said. "I had a feeling you'd be trouble when you tried fighting Mary's compulsion when she got you to drink the memory potion. And I only mean that in the best way. I've always been a bit of a troublemaker myself." Her eyes got a mischievous glint to them then, as if she was remembering a time long past.

I couldn't see the girl in front of me right now being a troublemaker... but something about that look told me she wasn't always this way.

I had so many questions for her. But right now I was too mad about what she'd done to me to think about anything else than getting her to admit she'd been wrong.

"You had no right to take my memories from me," I said, returning to the point. "You dropped me back home, completely clueless about the supernatural world. I knew something was off—that something awful had happened to me. But I didn't know what it was. Then Azazel took my mom, and I was thrown into this crazy supernatural world unprepared. If you hadn't taken my memories away, I might have been ready for what was coming. I might have been able to protect my mom."

"If I hadn't taken your memories away, you wouldn't have been able to return to a normal life," she countered.

"It might not seem like it now, but I was doing what was best for you."

How ridiculously condescending.

"You had no right to decide what was 'best for me,'" I said through clenched teeth. "You're not my mom. You don't even look like you're out of high school."

"I'm nineteen." She studied her hands, which were playing with the edges of her blanket. "At least I *was* nineteen before becoming immortal this winter."

"So you're younger than me." Despite my anger, I couldn't help feeling bad for her. Because whatever she'd been through until now, it had more than taken its toll.

But I needed to get back to the point—that she had no right to take my memories from me.

"Why did you do it?" I asked. "Why did you erase my memories when I asked you not to?"

"I just told you." She sighed, as if this conversation was exhausting her. "I wanted you to have a normal life."

"And look how that turned out." I glared at her. "You have no idea what I've been through these past few weeks."

"Yes, I do," she said. "Jacen told me everything."

"Right." I pressed my lips together—I should have figured he would. And truthfully, I was glad for it. The last thing I wanted was to rehash what had happened to

MICHELLE MADOW

me for the thousandth time. I'd done enough of that in the bunker and in the Haven.

But she needed to know what it had been like. From me—not from anyone else.

"I've been attacked by demons and have no idea how to fight them," I said. "I've been nearly killed multiple times. I was thrown into a bunker by demons, with no idea if I'd be able to escape. If it hadn't been for Noah and Sage, I'd be captured right now, just like my mom. Everything I've done since she disappeared has been to save her. *Everything.* Rosella told me to come here, enter the Angel Trials, and become a Nephilim. She promised that's how I could save my mom. Then I get here and learn everyone who's entered the Angel Trials has *died.* And now Violet wants me to take memory potion, leave Avalon, and forget everything that's happened to me? I swear, the only good thing that's happened these past few weeks has been Noah. If I didn't imprint on him, I'm pretty sure I would have lost it by now."

Honestly, I was pretty sure I was losing it now. Learning that the Angel Trials were a death sentence might have been my breaking point.

Maybe I shouldn't have come here. I should have gone to Noah instead.

Why did I think the Earth Angel would be able to fix things? I guess I'd expected her to apologize, or to tell

66

me there was another way. But seeing what a frail mess she was just made this all worse.

At some point when I was talking, the Earth Angel's eyes watered, like she was about to cry. I think it was when I mentioned the part about everyone dying. But I couldn't be sure.

She scooted over on the big bed, curled up her legs, and patted the empty spot next to her. "Come sit," she said gently. "It sounds like we have a lot to talk about."

"The last time we talked, you forced me to take memory potion," I said. "How do I know you won't do the same thing again?"

"I shouldn't have done that." She pressed her lips together, regret shining in her golden eyes. "I thought I was doing the right thing when I took your memories from you, but I was wrong. And you might be right that not knowing about the supernatural world made every-thing harder for you later. I don't know. But I *do* know that I made a mistake in making you take that memory potion, and I'm sorry for it."

"Really?" My mouth dropped open.

"Really," she said. "Why do you look so surprised?"

"I guess I didn't expect the Earth Angel of Avalon to apologize so easily."

She looked me over, as if seeing me in a new light. "I think we got off on the wrong foot," she finally said.

"Yeah." I rolled my eyes. "You could say that."

"So how about we start over?"

I couldn't believe we were having this conversation right now. "How do you want to do that?" I asked.

"To start, I don't want any formalities between us," she said. "Call me Annika."

"Okay." I shifted from one foot to another. "Are you sure?"

"Yes, I'm sure." She laughed, although it was kind of self-depreciating. "You didn't expect me to be like this, did you?"

"Not really," I admitted. "I thought you'd have wings and a halo and stuff. And that you'd be strong and scary."

"Oh, I'm strong—don't get me wrong there." She laughed again. "But scary? Not so much. Because yes, now I'm the Earth Angel of Avalon. But a few months ago, I was a human girl, just like you. I make mistakes all the time. And this whole supernatural world is new to me too. I'm doing my best, but recently it feels like my best just isn't enough." She shrugged, and I was surprised by her raw honesty. It was refreshing.

"All right, Annika," I said, testing the casual way she'd asked me to address her. It felt good—like I was talking to an equal. "I know you've heard about what happened to me from Jacen and maybe even from Mary. But do you want to hear about it from me?"

Sure, before I hadn't wanted to go through the details again. But now that she'd apologized and the line of communication was open between us, maybe it wouldn't be so bad to talk to her. Especially because she was the one who was supposed to be helping me save my mom... even if she didn't look capable of saving anyone right now.

"Yes." She motioned again to the empty spot on the bed next to her. "I'd like that very much."

And so, I plopped myself down next to her, made myself comfortable, and told her everything that had happened to me since the night of my birthday.

# RAVEN

*A*nnika and I must have sat there talking for over an hour. At some point, she'd had mana and hot chocolate brought in.

There were tears, hugs, and even a bit of laughter. There was even girl talk when I got to the part about imprinting on Noah and how frustratingly distant and moody he'd been in the beginning. Apparently, Annika and Jacen had had their share of troubles in the beginning of their relationship, too. She'd told me there was a *lot* more to that story, which she'd tell me about eventually. But right now, we were focusing on my long, crazy journey that had led me to Avalon.

"Now I finally get to Avalon, I'm ready to enter the Angel Trials, and Violet drops the bomb that no one has passed them yet," I finished. "That it's killing them all. I just... don't know what to do with that information." I pulled my legs up to my chest and wrapped my arms around them in a small attempt to comfort myself. It didn't work. I was still as scared as ever.

"Tell me about it." Annika sighed and buried her face in her palms. She dropped her hands down a second later and continued, "It's why I'm such a mess right now. These are my people. They trusted me, and they entered the Trials because they wanted to fight the demons. We went into the Angel Trials with such hope. Then the first candidate—one of the strongest to ever enter the Trials—completed all the initial tests with flying colors. His name was Toby. He proved he was ready to drink from the Holy Grail and accept the blessing of the angels. But he drank from the Grail, and he died. And he didn't just fall over peacefully. His death... it was brutal." She shuddered, and horror crossed her features, like she was watching his death all over again. Her golden eyes actually dimmed a bit.

"I'm sorry," I said the only thing that came to mind.

"At first, I thought it was a fluke," she continued, as if I wasn't even there. "I thought there was a reason Toby wasn't fit to be a Nephilim. That *is* the point of the Trials, after all. To determine who's destined to be a Nephilim or not. I figured there was something wrong with his inner self—something deeply ingrained that I hadn't been able to see—and that destiny knew best. And so, we continued on with the Trials as normal. But then the next human drank from the Grail—a girl named Hannah. She was good to the core, I know it. But she died too, just as painfully and as brutally as Toby. After her death, a handful of humans dropped out of the Trials. But most stayed, determined it would be different for them."

"They were strong," I said.

"Yes," she agreed. "And the Trials were all they had to live for. You see, most of the humans here came either from the Vale, or from a human area on Earth. Those who came from Earth tended to be lost and afraid. No family or friends—they lived on the streets, surviving by sheer grit and determination."

"How did you find them?" I asked.

"We sent scouts out," she said. "We needed to build an army, and had to start somewhere. Humans who were already fighters seemed like the best bet."

"Makes sense." I nodded.

"But they kept dying," she said. "At first I thought it had something to do with my blood, since that's what they were drinking from the Grail. I thought the pure angel blood was too strong for them to handle. So I tried diluting it. But when diluted, it did nothing. The only test left to do is have them drink Nephilim blood and see if they're able to handle it, but I can't test that when there are no Nephilim left. It's a catch twenty-two. And I'm honestly not sure if I have it in me to do any more tests at all. The guilt I felt each time they died…" Her eyes went distant again, and tears rolled down her cheeks. She turned away and wiped them from her face, as if she thought her tears were a weakness.

I got it. I hated crying in front of people, too.

"I can't imagine." I bit my lip, unsure how to continue. Comforting people who were crying wasn't one of my strengths in life.

But I had to say *something* more. It sounded like Annika had been through Hell and back. She looked like it, too. And while nothing could make it better, I had to try.

"It must have been so hard," I said. "You were doing what you thought you had to do to save the world. And at the end of the day, they chose to drink from the Grail. They believed in what everyone on Avalon is fighting for—ridding the demons from Earth. Their deaths weren't your fault."

"Logically, I understand that." She turned back to me, a glimmer of strength in her eyes that hadn't been there before. "But ever since becoming an angel, I *feel* more than I did before. When they died, it felt like a part of my heart died, too. I went to the mages about it, and apparently it's an angel thing. Angels have extreme empathy—it makes our emotions go on overdrive. It's why angels choose to live in Heaven and not come down to Earth. There's so much pain and sorrow on Earth. Angels would drown in their emotions. They'd be so lost it would make them useless. If it's this hard for me on Avalon—which is technically slightly removed from Earth—I can't imagine what it would be like going back there."

"That's why you holed yourself up in here?" I asked, looking around the chambers. The truth was, Annika didn't smell completely fresh—my guess would be that she hadn't showered in a few days. She'd clearly been hiding away in here. Probably reading, judging from the pile of books on her nightstand.

I recognized the book on top—it had been on my "to read" list back when everything was normal. I didn't get much time to read for fun between all my studying, but I'd planned on getting it in over summer break.

That old life of mine seemed so far away now.

"It is," she said. "I couldn't take seeing any more of the humans die. So I shut down the human training center in the academy, had them all take memory potion, and sent them back to Earth."

I flinched slightly when she said, "memory potion." She really liked wiping humans' memories, didn't she?

But I pressed my lips together, stopping myself from saying anything snarky. Annika was clearly in a rough place right now. Snarkiness wasn't going to help her feel better.

I *needed* her to feel better so she'd get her act together and figure out how to fix this.

"When was that?" I asked.

"A few weeks ago." She shrugged. "I've lost track of time."

Crap. This was *not* good. I needed to become a Nephilim to save my mom—and to save Sage and the others from Azazel. I couldn't do that if Annika wouldn't try to figure out what was killing everyone before me.

There had to be something she was missing. Some key to the puzzle.

"Was there anything similar about the humans who were dying?" I asked.

"No." She shook her head sadly. "Trust me, I've been over this multiple times. There's no pattern to the deaths. The only thing predictable is that every human who drinks from the Grail dies. Period."

"Did any gifted humans drink from the Grail?" The possibility that *this* was the answer lit my chest up with excitement. Maybe regular humans weren't strong enough to survive drinking from the Grail, no matter what.

"They did," she said, and I instantly deflated. "Two of them. They died, too."

"What were their gifts?"

She scratched her head, as if trying to remember. "Flexibility and… the ability to eat anything without gaining weight."

"Seriously?" My eyes widened, distracted for a moment. "That's an actual gift?"

"It is." Annika smiled—a sad, wistful smile, but still a smile. "It wasn't particularly useful on Avalon since mana fuels the body purely with what it needs, but she loved bragging about how she could put down insane quantities of food without gaining a pound. I think she made popular YouTube videos about it back on Earth."

"I thought you recruited humans from the streets?" I asked.

"And from the Vale," she said. "This girl—Kacy—had been brought to the Vale a few years before me. We knew each other in passing. I really thought she'd have the strength to pass the Trials. But she didn't. Even though she was gifted, she died like the rest of them."

"There must be something you're missing." I spoke faster now, trying to keep the panic from rising up in my voice. I didn't come all the way to Avalon just to be told that the Angel Trials were impossible. "Some other reason why the humans are all dying. There has to be a way to fix this. The supernaturals on Earth are counting on you. The *world* is counting on you."

"You think I don't know that?" She stared straight at me, her gaze sharper now. "I've been trying to figure it out for weeks. I've found nothing. I'm going to keep my team searching for an explanation, because there has to be an answer out there somewhere. But until we find it, I think it's best that you take memory potion and go back home."

"Seriously?" I couldn't believe what I was hearing right now. "First of all, memory potion doesn't work on me. Secondly, I came here to become a Nephilim. I have to save my mom. And I *will* save my mom. Rosella said as much. Maybe you don't believe me, but you believe Rosella. Right?"

"Rosella didn't say when you'd be able to become a Nephilim," Annika said sadly. "It might not happen for years, for all we know."

"No." I clenched my fists, digging my nails into my palms. "I won't accept that."

"You really are stubborn," she said with a small chuckle.

"It's not funny." I glared at her. "None of this is funny."

"You think I don't know that?" Her tone was as scathing as my own. "One by one, I watched my people die. Be stubborn all you want, but you didn't see it. The way my blood poisoned them from the inside, welting their skin and making them cough up their organs until there was nothing left but pieces of them on the ground. The way they clawed at themselves to make the pain go away and begged for someone to help them. But nothing helped. Nothing but death."

I hadn't wanted to know the details of how they'd died. It sounded more horrifying than I'd imagined. But I stayed strong, determined not to let it shake me. Now wasn't the time for that.

"You're right—I don't know what it was like to watch that," I said. "But you don't know what it's like out there on Earth. Azazel is kidnapping gifted humans and doing who knows what with them. He's turned the entire Montgomery pack into demon bound slaves. He's a monster, and he needs to be stopped. But only a Nephilim or angel can kill a greater demon. So with no Nephilim here on Avalon, I guess you'll just have to go to Earth and kill him yourself."

"I can't do that," Annika said softly.

"Why?" I asked. "Because it's too difficult for you to go to Earth with your angel empathy thing?" If that was it, she needed to suck it up. And I had no problem being the one to tell her that.

"That's not it," she said. "Yes, it would be difficult for me to go to Earth with my 'angel empathy thing.' But I'm stronger than you realize."

"Then what is it?"

"I'm bound to Avalon," she said. "When I arrived on this island, it was dead. Then I signed a contract with my blood and brought it back to life. Doing so bonded a piece of my soul with Avalon to bring it to its current glory. It blessed the island and made it impossible to locate. If I leave, so does the blessing that hides Avalon. Everyone here will be exposed and at risk. The demons will attack, and if they attack now... I'm not confident we have the strength to beat them."

"So you're just going to let Azazel get away with it?" I backed away from her, infuriated. "You're not going to try stopping him?"

"I'm going to stop him," she said. "Just not yet."

"If not now, then when?"

"Once I figure out what's going wrong with the Trials," she said. "Once humans are able to drink from the Grail and survive to become Nephilim. Once I start forming my army. Then, once all that is complete, I can think about defeating the greater demons. That's how this war against the demons is going to be fought, and eventually won. One slow step at a time. It might take years, but we'll get there. We *have* to get there. Otherwise, everything I've been through until now will have been for nothing. And I can't accept that. I *won't* accept that."

Her golden eyes glowed brighter with each word she spoke. Finally, Annika was showing some of the confidence and determination I'd expected from the Earth Angel. It wasn't what I'd wanted to hear, but it was better than nothing.

I could work with this, and with her. I had no other choice.

But I couldn't become a Nephilim.

I leaned against the frame of the bed, frustrated and lost and confused all at once. How was I supposed to save my mom—and Sage—if I couldn't enter the Trials and become a Nephilim?

It didn't make any sense.

Then, when the helplessness of the situation felt like it was too much to handle, I remembered what Rosella had told me back in the Haven.

*Whatever you learn when you get to Avalon—no matter how hopeless or impossible things might seem—you must always believe in yourself. You have a gift, Raven. When you put your mind to something, you can accomplish anything. Don't ever forget that.*

All at once, it clicked into place. Rosella had been trying to warn me. She knew Annika's secret—that every human who had entered the Trials so far had died. Of course she knew. She was a psychic.

She knew, and she'd reminded me of my gift. Stubbornness. Determination. A drive to succeed no matter what. A drive to *live*.

The others might have died after drinking angel blood from the Grail. But I would survive.

At least, I'd try.

"What are you thinking about?" Annika asked.

I swallowed, knowing she was going to think I was crazy. "Rosella sent me to Avalon to enter the Angel Trials and become a Nephilim," I said. "Before I came here, she spoke with me again in the Haven. She told me that when I got to Avalon, I'd learn something that would make it feel like my quest was impossible. Then she reminded me about my gift. About how it allows me to accomplish what others can't. She told me that no matter what, I needed to believe in myself."

"No..." Annika shook her head, like she knew what I was going to say next.

She was scared for me. I couldn't blame her. I was scared for myself, too.

"Yes," I cut her off before she could say more. "You trust Rosella, don't you?"

"I do," she said without a second thought. "I wouldn't be here today if not for her guidance."

"Well, Rosella sent me here to enter the Angel Trials, drink from the Grail, and become the first Nephilim in your army," I said. "So that's exactly what I'm going to do."

After my long chat with Annika, the Earth Angel had Camelia send for Violet.

The mage teleported to the room within seconds and fluffed out her purple medieval gown. She and her sisters were the only ones I'd seen wearing gowns around the castle. I guessed it was a mage thing.

"Your Highness," Violet said to Annika, dipping into a curtsy.

Annika rolled her eyes. "I told them they don't need to be so formal," she said to me. "But they insist." She flashed me a conspiratorial smile, and I gave her one right back.

If someone had told me a few hours ago that the Earth Angel and I were going to start becoming *friends*, I never would have believed them.

The world was so weird sometimes.

Violet simply stood there and waited for a command from Annika. If she was shocked by the Earth Angel's messy appearance, she did a good job at hiding it.

"Please escort Raven to the human quarters in the academy and help get her situated," Annika said to Violet. "She's going to begin training for the Angel Trials tomorrow."

The calm, pleasant look that seemed to be permanently plastered on Violet's face fell to one of complete shock. "But the human quarters are closed," she sputtered, looking from Annika to me and back to Annika again. "The Angel Trials are cancelled."

"They *were* cancelled." Annika sat straighter, sounding like a leader for the first time since I met her. "But I'm opening them again. For Raven only."

Violet pressed her lips together, like she had some serious words to speak to the Earth Angel. But whatever was going through her mind, she must have contained it. "Very well," she said simply, looking to me. "I was just about to fetch Jessica to get her situated in the academy's vampire quarters. Since all the academy quarters are in the same building, we can pick her up on our way there."

"Perfect." Annika beamed at her, and then turned to

me. "It was wonderful to meet you—again. I'll see you tonight at the welcome banquet."

"Do I need anything fancy for this banquet?" I glanced at Violet's gown and motioned to the Haven whites I was still wearing. "Because this is all I have."

"The academy will provide you with everything you need," Violet said, her tone back to serene and calm. "Now, come along. Jessica's waiting, and we don't have any time to waste."

Violet led me to a turret similar to the one where she'd given me my orientation, except at the other end of the castle.

"Why are we walking everywhere?" I asked on our way there. "Don't you have the ability to teleport?"

"I do," she said. "But it's important that you get your bearings around here. You won't always have a mage or a witch by your side."

She led the way up the stairs of a spiral tower similar to the one from earlier. When we reached the door at the top, she knocked.

The door slammed open—right into her—and Noah rushed out in a blur. He reached for my hands, looking down at me with fear, worry, and love in his eyes.

"Dahlia told us about the Angel Trials," he said. "If you're leaving, I'm going with you. We can go back to the Haven and talk to Rosella. There *has* to be another way to save your mom and Sage."

"Noah," I cut him off, speaking his name slowly. I felt his panic radiating through the imprint bond. "I'm not leaving."

"You're not?" His brows furrowed in confusion.

"You remember what Rosella told me in the Haven, right?" I asked. "That no matter how impossible things seemed here on Avalon, I needed to believe in myself? That my gift allows me to defeat crazy odds?"

"Of course I remember," he said. "But those Trials... they'll kill you."

"They won't." I stood strongly, determined to make it true just by speaking the words. "Using your slicer to kill a demon should have killed me, but I survived. The same way that I'll survive the Angel Trials. By using my gift."

"Are you two done here?" Violet looked between Noah and me impatiently. "The Earth Angel has tasked me to bring Raven and Jessica to their appropriate quarters in the academy."

Noah turned to Violet and puffed out his chest, towering over her. "I'm coming with you," he said.

"No, you are not," Dahlia trilled from their orientation room. "We're not finished with your orientation yet!"

Noah ignored her and continued giving Violet his intense wolf stare down.

If he intimidated her, she didn't let it show. "The Earth Angel specifically asked me to bring Raven and Jessica to their appropriate quarters in the academy," she repeated. "If you have any grievances against this arrangement, you can bring it up with the Earth Angel at the banquet tonight."

"I have 'grievances' against more than Raven's sleeping arrangement," he growled at her, before refocusing on me. "What do you want to do?" he asked.

"I want to go to the academy," I said honestly.

"How far is this academy from here?"

"Not far at all," Violet answered happily. "It's right behind the castle."

Noah took a deep breath, tension tight through his body. "Fine," he muttered. "Go get your tour of the academy. We'll talk later."

His words were heavy, and they held a lot of meaning—both that I could hear in his tone and feel through the bond. He didn't want me entering the Trials. He thought it was too dangerous. He couldn't bear the thought of me drinking from the Grail and dying.

"Deal." I squeezed his hand for assurance. "I'll be safe. I promise."

"Don't make promises you can't keep."

I swallowed, because he was right. When I told him I'd be safe, I meant I'd be safe for the night. As for through the Angel Trials... who knew what would happen?

The world suddenly felt like it was swirling around me, and I blinked to steady myself. I needed to take this one step at a time. If I thought too far ahead, the terror of what I was doing would consume me. Right now, I needed to focus on the present.

Which meant going with Violet to get situated at the human quarters in the academy.

# RAVEN

*V*iolet led Jessica and me through the hall of the first floor of the castle, pointing at doors and telling us where they led as we walked. We'd passed the ballroom, dining room, kitchens, library, meeting room, throne room, and a few other rooms Violet had rattled off the names of while hurrying us along.

I definitely lost track of which room was where. Judging from the bewildered look in Jessica's eyes as she looked around the castle, she felt just as lost as I did.

One thing I *did* notice was that besides a handful of people who scurried by, the castle was nearly empty.

"Where is everyone?" I asked.

"Training or working," Violet answered. "Here at Avalon, we're preparing for a war—not lounging about hosting tea parties. Everyone has duties they must perform during the day."

"I guess the training doesn't happen in the castle," I said.

"Of course not." Violet raised her chin and sniffed, as if my comment had insulted her. "We don't want to damage the property."

Right. Of course.

She led us out into a beautiful courtyard, with a stone fountain in the center and trees in full bloom at the height of spring. Birds chirped everywhere, and the scent of fresh flowers filled the air. But I didn't have much time to admire the gardens, because Violet rushed us through to the largest door on the other side. It led us through the back area of the castle and out into the open.

Behind the castle were luscious, green hills that appeared to go on forever. There were clusters of little cottages along them. But I barely paid attention to those. Because right at the top of one of the tallest, nearby hills was a massive, imposing, stone manor house. It was at four stories high, with a thatched roof, and was at least twice as wide as it was tall. Who knew how far it went in the back. A dirt road led from where we stood at the back of the castle toward the manor.

"This is the training house," Violet said, looking at

the manor with pride. "Or Avalon Academy, as we've started calling it."

"That's the school?" Jessica squeaked, looking more intimidated than when we were walking through the castle. I couldn't blame her. When I thought of a school, I imagined typical boxy buildings and dorms. Not a literal *mansion*.

"Follow me." Violet continued forward, clearly taking Jessica's question as rhetorical. "The students are all training right now. But they'll be back before sunset, so let's get the two of you settled before they arrive."

The double door entrance opened to a massive and ornate foyer. Everything was so traditional and grand, and as I looked around, I felt like I'd walked straight into a Jane Austen novel. The giant manor made the Montgomery pack's compound in the Hollywood Hills look small.

Violet led us up the grand staircase and then down the hall to the left. She pushed open a majestic wooden door, leading us into a big, long room with beds lining the walls. Hardwood floors, sparkling chandeliers, and open curtains that let the light flood inside made the entire space feel warm and welcoming.

"This is the female vampire dormitory." Violet smiled proudly, as if she'd designed the room herself.

Each bed was full sized and situated under a half canopy that jutted out from the above wall. The canopies gave each bed a feeling of privacy, even though there had to be over twenty beds in all. Slightly more than half of them had unique comforters on them, along with matching canopies.

Large wardrobes sat next to each bed, and there were also big trunks at the feet. It was downright heavenly compared to what we'd been forced to endure in the bunker.

The beds with colored comforters had nightstands with books and other knickknacks on them. Other than that, the room was perfectly organized and tidy.

"The open beds are the ones with white comforters," Violet continued. "Jessica, please choose which one you'd like to be yours."

Most of the beds that were taken were closer to the windows, whereas most of the open ones were closest to the door. Apparently the windows were prime real estate.

"I'll take that one." Jessica pointed to the next open bed in the line. It was the obvious choice—I would have made it too. Because choosing a bed far away from the others would have been a terrible way to make friends on the first day.

"Perfect." Violet smiled. "Now, sit down on it to claim it."

"Is this some kind of vampire thing?" Jessica asked. "I need to put my scent on the bed?"

"Something like that," Violet said.

Jessica walked over to the bed and sat on it. The moment she placed her palms down on it, all of the bedding—the comforter, pillows, and canopy—changed to deep purple tie-dye.

She gasped, looking at the bed in shock. "It's the same as my bed from home," she said, turning to Violet with wonder. "I missed my bed so much. How did it know?"

"Mage magic," Violet said with a twinkle in her eye. "My sisters and I designed the spell ourselves. Check out the wardrobe, too."

She did—it was full of her favorite clothes. It also had a week's worth of the academy's plain black uniform with a small "A" insignia on the front left side, which Violet told us was to always be worn during training hours.

"The trunks are for your dirty clothes," Violet continued, pointing to the carved wooden trunk at the foot of Jessica's bed. "The housekeepers come by twice a week to get your laundry."

"You mean there's a spell for making all of our stuff appear in our wardrobes, but there's no spell to do laundry?" I asked.

"Of course not." Violet shuddered, as if the mere suggestion was disgusting. "Nothing gets clothes clean like a good old fashioned washing and drying."

Both Jessica and I shared a look of confusion. Magic was weird.

"Now, stop sitting around," Violet said to Jessica. "Get changed, and we can show Raven to her quarters."

## RAVEN

The human quarters were one floor up. By the time we were there, my legs were sore from all the steps I'd done today—back in the castle, and now here.

"Why make the humans do the extra set of steps when the vampires and shifters have supernatural strength?" I asked once we reached the top.

"As a human training on Avalon, you need to be building your strength," Violet explained. "We consider every way to help you do that, even if it's as simple as putting an extra set of stairs in your daily routine."

"Good to know," I said as she led us down the opposite wing of the manor. It felt like we were going as far away from the vampire quarters as possible.

The door leading to the human quarters looked the

same as the one to the vampire quarters. But inside the room, the curtains were shut, and all of the furniture was covered with plain white sheets. The only light came in from the hallway.

It was like a creepy haunted mansion.

"Sorry about that," Violet said nervously. "I forgot we had the furniture covered to preserve it for when we reopened these quarters." Quickly, she rushed to the nearest bed and pulled the sheet off of it. She did the same for the wardrobe and trunk for that bed, before moving on to remove the sheets from the chandeliers and open the curtains. The sunlight poured in, revealing a thin layer of dust blanketing everything in the room.

A hollow pit settled at the bottom of my stomach at the thought of staying in this big, quiet room by myself.

Each empty bed in these quarters had once slept a human who had pledged themselves to Avalon, entered the Angel Trials, and died instead of becoming a Nephilim.

"No need to worry about... all of this." Violet motioned around the deserted room. "I'll send the housekeepers in to fix it up while I give the two of you the grand tour. When we return it'll be good as new. In the meantime, why don't you claim your bed so you can change into clothes of your own?"

"I don't want that bed." I glanced at the bed she'd

randomly chosen for me, looking instead to the one closest to the window. "I want that one."

"Of course." Violet's cheeks turned red, and she hurried to the bed I'd pointed to, removing the sheets from it and its surrounding furniture. "Here you go." She tossed the sheets to the side—I supposed for the housekeepers to get later—and gave me an encouraging smile. "It's all yours."

I walked over to the bed, sat down on it, and placed my palms on the plushy mattress. The moment I did, the bedding and canopy changed from white into a stunning, patterned, silk gold.

"Wow," I said, taking in the regal-looking bed. "That's definitely not my bedding from home."

"The magic can sense what you need," Violet explained. "Jessica got her bedding from home because she needed the comfort of it. You, apparently, needed something else."

"Apparently," I agreed, although I wasn't sure what that something was. This bed was fit for a queen. Not for a human getting ready to enter the Angel Trials and potentially die.

I swallowed at the reminder and looked to the wardrobe, needing to think about something else. "I wonder what clothes I got," I said, walking over to the closet and throwing open the doors.

Along with a bunch of the required black training uniforms, my favorite clothes waited for me in the dresser. Jeans I'd had since high school, t-shirts, tank tops, shorts, and my most comfortable sneakers and flats. The wardrobe appeared to be endless—or at least larger than it looked from the outside.

I was able to prop the wardrobe door in a way that gave me just enough privacy while I changed. There was even a hairbrush inside so I could smooth out my tangled hair. Once I was in jeans, a tank top, and comfortable flats, I closed the door and walked toward Violet and Jessica.

"All right," I said. "I'm ready for the tour."

"Wait," Jessica said before Violet could take a step toward the exit.

Both the mage and I looked at her to continue.

"Raven shouldn't have to stay in here all alone," she said, gazing around the stark, empty room. "I want to live in the human quarters, too."

"Really?" I smiled at my friend, humbled at the gesture. Of course I wanted her to stay with me. But I also didn't want to stop her from bonding with the other vampires. "Are you sure?"

"Definitely," she said, but she was cut off by Violet.

"Absolutely not." The mage looked at Jessica like she'd said something insane.

"What?" Jessica stumbled a step backward—she certainly hadn't anticipated *that* response. "Why not?"

"You're a vampire," Violet said. "Raven's a human. Staying here with her puts her in danger."

"Seriously?" I rolled my eyes. "As if I'm not *already* in danger by entering the Angel Trials?"

"Exactly." Violet's expression hardened. "Thus a reason not to put you in any *more* danger. Jessica is a vampire—a newly turned one at that. What happens if she loses control—even for a second—and decides to feed from you?"

"That won't happen," I said, although I knew Violet's point made sense. "She's my friend."

"And you're her food," Violet reminded me. "Absolutely not. I can't even believe we're having this discussion."

"I have excellent control over my bloodlust." Jessica stood straighter and looked Violet straight in the eye. "Mary said so herself."

"I don't care what Mary said," Violet said. "That was on the Haven. This is Avalon. We have rules here. One of those rules is that students at the academy must dorm with their same species, and same gender. There are reasons for these rules. And even if I wanted to let one person break them—which I don't—I wouldn't do it.

Make one exception, and everyone will want one. So no. Absolutely not."

While I hated to admit it, Violet *did* have a point.

"Thanks for trying," I said to Jessica, giving her a small shrug. "But I'll be fine here alone. It'll be great, actually. After how cramped we all were in the bunker, I'm happy to have a room to myself." I forced a smile to drive the point home.

She crossed her arms and narrowed her eyes at me, not having it.

Duh. Her gift was the ability to tell lies from the truth.

"Seriously?" She raised an eyebrow in disbelief. "You think that works on me?"

"I guess not." I focused instead on a *real* reason why it wasn't good for her to room with me. "But Violet's right. We just got here. It'll be hard enough for me to fit in as the only human at the school. There's no need to make you an outcast as well for living with me."

"At least one of you has some sense." Violet swung her dress around, shaking her hips as she made her way to the exit of the room. "Now, are you both coming?" she asked. "We have a lot of ground to cover, and I want to make sure you have your bearings before the other students return from training."

## NOAH

*O*nce Dahlia completed our orientation, she looked around the table at Thomas, Bella, and me. "If you all are finished with your food, I can show you to your quarters," she said, standing up and straightening her dress.

It was just a formality, since we'd finished eating and drinking a while ago.

"I want to stay with Raven." I stared straight at her, not leaving it up for discussion.

"I'm afraid that won't be possible," she said. "Only students can live in the academy. *But* I think you'll be pleased with what I arranged for you…"

She smiled and waggled her eyebrows, practically begging me to ask for more. After a few seconds, I couldn't take it.

"What have you 'arranged for me?'" I asked, quoting her directly.

"There are shifters from the Vale living in the cottages near the castle—which also happen to be close to the academy manor where Raven will be staying," she said. "I believe some of them are from your pack..." She tilted her head, clearly dangling a carrot in front of my face and getting joy from it.

"I was in the Southern Vale pack," I said, unable to resist chasing the carrot. "Are the surviving members here?"

My pack had been in the front lines at the war in the Vale. Not many had survived. I'd felt through the pack bond when each of them had died. And of the ones that had survived, I'd left for my quest before finding out if they'd decided to go to Avalon or remain in the Vale.

I hadn't wanted to know their decision. Because if they'd stayed in the Vale, I might have stayed, too.

Not that they likely would have wanted me to stay. I'd fallen for a demon's tricks and gotten us involved in a deadly war that got many of us killed. If my pack had wanted to throw me out, I wouldn't have blamed them.

The supernatural community as a whole still generally looked down upon me—the infamous First Prophet of the Vale. I swear, I'd never be able to get rid of that awful title. Hopefully completing the Earth Angel's quest and making it to Avalon would do the trick. But only time would tell.

"There are members of the Southern Vale pack living in Avalon," Dahlia confirmed. "They have a cottage behind the castle. Would you like me to take you there?"

"Yes." I stood up, not needing to be asked twice.

"I thought so." She smiled. "First we'll show Thomas and Bella to their rooms in the castle, and then the two of us will continue on back to the wolf village. I'm sure your pack will be thrilled to see you again."

I wished I could be as sure as she was.

"The banquet is this evening, after the sun sets and once true night begins," Dahlia said as she led us down the castle hall. "Everyone will be there, including the Earth Angel."

"What time is that, exactly?" Thomas was unemotional and distant. He'd been that way since Dahlia broke the news that none of the humans had survived the Angel Trials and that Annika couldn't leave Avalon.

I didn't think he was planning on staying on Avalon until Raven came by and told us she was still going to enter the Trials. Now, all hope for freeing Sage was on Raven.

I'd have to keep my eye on Thomas. He was going to want to push Raven so she'd hurry up and become a Nephilim as quickly as possible. I couldn't allow that to happen.

Truthfully, I didn't want Raven to enter the Trials at all. I hated that she'd be putting her life at risk.

I wished I could do it instead. But only humans could become Nephilim. Which meant we were all counting on her.

Deep down, I believed she could do it. I'd seen how stubborn she was. And I trusted that Rosella wouldn't have steered us astray.

I just wished I wasn't so damn scared for her.

"Like all technology, clocks don't work here on Avalon," Dahlia told Thomas. "We plan our schedule based on the patterns of the sun and moon."

"Then I see I have my first task here set out for myself," he said. "Because you all need a more practical way to keep track of time."

"Let us know what equipment you'll need," she said. "We'll make sure you have it."

She showed Thomas and Bella to their rooms in the castle, which were fit for royalty. King beds with canopies, private bathrooms, and the works. They both appeared satisfied with their accommodations, looking immediately at home.

But I understood why the shifters wanted to live somewhere else. Our animal sides craved to live close to nature. Being holed up in a stone room in a castle would feel suffocating after a while.

"I take it the redhead is your girlfriend?" Dahlia asked as she led me across the courtyard.

"We're imprinted on each other." Calling Raven my *girlfriend* was far too casual a term for what she meant to me.

"Lucky girl." Dahlia smirked, her eyes roaming up and down my body.

"Yes." I walked further away from her, making my disinterest clear. Not that I should have needed to—she knew Raven and I were together. But from the glint in Dahlia's eyes, she liked to play games. And I wasn't having it. "She is."

We walked in silence until reaching the back wall of the castle. There, Dahlia pushed open a large door, and we walked through an arched hall to exit the castle grounds.

Once outside, I saw the giant manor house and the clusters of wooden cottages around it. The cottages were built into the sides of the hills, surrounded by plants and trees. Warm and welcoming, they were a part of the nature around them.

Even if I hadn't picked up on the noticeable woodsy

smell of shifters, I would have known they lived here. Because in my heart, it felt like home.

"Usually everyone's working or training during this time of day," Dahlia said, gazing out at the village. "But we know how important it is for shifters to be greeted by their pack, so we sent a fire message out to the packs to notify them about your arrival. They should be waiting for you inside. I believe their cottage is—"

"That one," I interrupted, bursting into my wolf form and running toward the cottage before she could get out the rest of her sentence.

*I*t felt freeing to run as a wolf again. Ever since going on the demon hunt, I'd been so consumed with killing demons that I hadn't had any time to just *be*. Yes, I had my motorcycle rides through the Hollywood Hills, but that held nothing to running as a wolf.

I could have run the entire length of the island, so it felt like I reached the cottage far too quickly. Once there, I stared at the door, my heart pounding. Because I had no idea how my pack was going to greet me.

I'd been so happy to see them again that I'd run toward their cottage without a second thought. But there was a good chance they hadn't forgiven me for my involvement in the war at the Vale. Plus, I'd deserted them to go off on my demon hunt. They had no obligation to take me back.

I needed to prepare myself for the possibility that they might send me away. Back to being a lone wolf.

I'd handled it for the past few weeks. I could handle it again. Especially now that Raven and I had each other.

I shifted back into human form and raised my hand to knock. Since I was still wearing my cloaking ring, my pack mates were unable to smell me like I could smell them.

It was generally considered rude for supernaturals to wear cloaking rings while not on missions, because it allowed us to hide from others. Plus, cloaking rings were expensive. There was no reason to invest in one unless you had something to hide. So anyone wearing a cloaking ring was immediately viewed with suspicion.

But I had no home right now, so I had nowhere to safely keep the ring except for on my body. Which meant I had to announce my arrival the human way.

I knocked, trying to ignore the way my stomach was jumping into my throat, and bracing myself for the worst. My pack mates were either going to accept me or not. Either way, I'd deal with it and find my place on Avalon.

The door swung open, revealing Sarah's familiar face.

Sarah was one of the eldest members of the Southern Vale pack. Her skin was saggy and wrinkled, but her eyes gleamed with the happiness of a much younger woman. And much to my surprise, when she saw me, she smiled.

"Noah!" she exclaimed, moving aside and motioning for me to come in. "We've been expecting you."

I stepped inside the cottage, looking around to assess the situation. The living room was warm and cozy, with couches surrounding a blazing fireplace. There were six others on the sofas. The moment I walked inside, they all stood up.

Four of them were children. Pre-teens, really. Timothy, Aaron, Rebecca, and Naomi. They were our four strongest young fighters, and everyone said had the most potential once they grew older. They each looked up at me with a mix of fear and respect. Which I supposed was better than the loathing I'd anticipated.

A woman and a man stood alongside them. The woman—Esther—was around the same age my mother would have been if my parents hadn't been killed when I was young during one of the many fights for land that the packs of the Vale had amongst each other. A kind, empathetic woman, Esther was the storyteller of the pack. What she lacked in physical prowess, she made up for in the magical way she could weave words and captivate with a tale. As a child, I remembered huddling around campfires for hours on cold, snowy nights to listen to her stories.

The man was Gabriel. Other than myself, he was one of the best fighters in the Vale. We used to train together all the time. Avalon was lucky to have him in their army.

Everyone in the cottage had their feet slightly angled toward Gabriel, tipping me off that he was the alpha of what remained of the pack.

Then, the unexpected happened.

Gabriel locked his gaze on mine and kneeled. The others followed suit.

I stared back at them, shocked. Because I'd seen this happen before. Why were they doing it now?

"First Prophet," Gabriel started, speaking the words as a compliment instead of the curse they'd been. "We know about the quest the Earth Angel sent you on to slay ten demons and make up for your sins. Congratulations on completing your mission. Now, just as Avalon has accepted you onto the island, we accept you back into the pack. And I invite you to take your rightful place as alpha."

I was shocked into silence. Most of what he'd said was exactly what I'd hoped would happen when I was reunited with the remainder of my pack on Avalon.

Except for that last part.

Because I was no alpha. I wasn't always the best

follower, either, but I'd never seen myself as a leader. I was more of a lone wolf, always on the outside looking in.

But they were all looking at me, waiting for a response. I needed to either accept or decline. That was how this worked.

Well, at least it was how it worked when an alpha offered the spot to another pack member. There was always the option to challenge the alpha to a fight to the death to take his place as well. In those cases, the winner became the new alpha. But this—giving up the position freely—was different.

Now, I had a choice to make. One I wasn't prepared for in the slightest.

"This is all that's left?" I asked, looking around at the seven of them. Our pack had twenty-four members before the Battle at the Vale. I'd known most hadn't survived, since I'd felt their deaths in battle. But seeing the pack whittled down to fewer than half of that made my chest feel hollow. Like losing pieces of myself.

"There are five still at the Vale," Sarah said, rattling off the names of my fellow pack mates who'd stayed behind. Three of them were children, which made sense, since children didn't fight on the front line in the battle. "They weren't accepted onto Avalon, so they're making a home in the Vale under King Alexander's peaceful reign," she continued, sadness flashing over her eyes before she said the next part. "As you know, the others didn't make it."

I glanced at the floor, taking a moment of silence to remember my fallen pack mates.

We'd thought we were going to decimate the vampires in the Battle at the Vale. Which we did. Fewer shifters had died in the battle than vampires. But war was a terrible, ugly thing. No side ever came out unscathed.

And with so many demons released from the Hell Gate, it was only going to get worse from here.

"Well?" Gabriel looked at me, his trusting brown eyes round with hope. "What do you say? Will you be our new alpha?"

"You've been alpha since the group of you arrived on Avalon." I said it as a statement, not a question.

"I have." He nodded.

"So why give the spot to me?"

"I know I always put up a good fight when we sparred, but we both know you're the better fighter of the two of us," he said with a chuckle. He was correct, so I said nothing. "Plus, you've killed ten demons. We've been here on Avalon since the Battle at the Vale. Yes, we've been training, but we've yet to be on the field. No one on Avalon has."

"So everyone here is doing what?" I asked. "Sitting around training and letting the demons kill whoever they want to on Earth?"

"That's the strange thing," Esther piped in. "The demons on Earth are laying low. The humans there are clueless that anything has changed."

"Except for the gifted humans the demons are kidnapping," I said. "*They* know it's changed."

"The demons are planning something," Sarah said. "We all know it. The leaders here are trying to figure out what that something is before we launch a full-scale attack. In the meantime, our warriors are training every day so we're ready when that time comes."

"And what's your position here on Avalon?" I asked, since Sarah was far too old to be useful in battle. She'd once been talented with her teeth and claws, but now that she was over a century old, age had taken her dexterity away from her. It was why she'd survived the Battle at the Vale. We'd had her stay back with the children, knowing the battlefield was no place for her anymore.

"Being old doesn't make me useless," she said with a smile, her tone making it clear that she knew I knew that. "My physical strength might have faded, but I used to be able to take down nearly any challenger in a fight. That knowledge is still up here." She pointed to her head. "I oversee the shifter training sessions, giving advice not just to the trainees, but to the trainers as well."

I nodded, since she'd done the same on the Vale when we were preparing for war with the vampires. But there was one part that still didn't make sense...

"How did you make it through the simulation to get onto the island?" I asked. "No offense. It's just that the simulation required strength and endurance."

Yes, there were ways to get through the simulation without having to enter a physical fight, like Raven and I had done. But there was still the long trek in the beginning from the cave to the stream where we'd met the unicorn and wyvern—the trek where we'd been deprived of food and water. And a shifter's final years of life were the hardest. Our species entered a rapid decline during that time, making them weaker than a human and fully dependent on the pack. It was no secret that Sarah had entered her final years. She no longer had the energy to survive even the long walk in the simulation.

"Ah, the simulation," she said, a strange peace setting in her expression. "When I opened my eyes in the cave, I was young again. King Arthur returned me to my prime so I could show him what I was truly made of. Unfortunately, when I woke back up on my boat floating toward

Avalon, I was back to the way I am now. Not even King Arthur or the mystical island of Avalon has the power to reverse the effects of time. Pause them, yes. But reverse them? No."

I nodded, knowing she was referring to the immortality granted to us by the mana and Holy Water.

"We'll fill you in on the details of our arrivals here and our lives here later," Gabriel said, shifting impatiently on his knee. "But right now, you need to stop putting off your decision. You're the only one in our pack who's fought a demon and lived to tell the tale. And you didn't just kill one demon—you killed *ten* of them. So do you want to take your rightful place as alpha or not?"

They were looking at me with such hope. Especially the children.

Back in the Vale, I'd never considered becoming alpha. There were others who had been born and bred for the role. I was a talented fighter, yes, but that was all. Then I'd assumed a leadership role as the First Prophet, and we all knew how *that* turned out.

But now that we were on Avalon, circumstances had changed. And Gabriel was right. I wasn't the same person I'd been before leaving on my quest. I now had the experience my pack needed to respect me as their leader.

Most surprisingly of all, now that I was faced with the opportunity, it felt wrong to say no.

"Yes," I said, and they all simultaneously let out a breath of relief. "I accept the position of alpha of the Southern Vale pack."

"Perfect." Gabriel stood up and shook my hand. His grip was firm, but he lowered his gaze before I did mine. It was a sign of respect. "Let's get my stuff out of the master bedroom and get you moved in."

RAVEN

The academy tour was mostly of the first floor, as the other floors were used for living quarters. Violet told us about the daily routine at the academy. Waking up early, mealtimes, training times, etc. Afternoons were spent learning the history of the supernatural world, battle strategy, etiquette while dealing with different supernatural creatures, and basic academic stuff like that. Mornings were for fight training.

From the way Violet looked me over when she mentioned fight training, I could tell she didn't think I was going to be able to handle it well.

I couldn't wait to prove her wrong.

Once the tour was over, Violet led us out to the front

door. There, we waited for the other students to arrive back at the house.

Right after the bottom of the sun touched the horizon, wyverns and unicorns came flying and running over the crest of the tallest hill in the distance. There must have been over a hundred of them in all. While they were only specks, I saw people riding on their backs. And they were heading straight toward us. With the sun setting behind them, it looked like a scene straight out of a fairy tale.

My heart warmed at the sight of the magical creatures. It was beautiful moments like this one where none of this felt real.

"You didn't mention there were *unicorns* on Avalon," I said, gazing out at them in awe. I focused on the unicorns because they were close to my heart after the simulation, although wyverns were cool, too.

"I figured I'd let you see for yourself." Violet smiled as she looked out at the incoming creatures. "Everyone on Avalon has either a unicorn or wyvern companion to help them get around the island. You met yours during the simulation to see if you were worthy of coming here or not."

"Annar." I gave a little jump of excitement as I said her name. Jessica looked equally as excited at the thought of seeing her unicorn, Clover, again. "You mean she's here?"

"She is," Violet confirmed. "At least, she'll be here when you need her."

"What do you mean by that?"

"The unicorns and wyverns don't live on Avalon," she said. "They're from my realm—Mystica. But each unicorn or wyvern has a magical connection with the human companion they bonded with in the simulation. They know when and where to pop in to give you transportation whenever you need it. You'll both be reunited with either your unicorn or wyvern tomorrow, when you head out to your first training session."

"Wow." Jessica gazed out toward the creatures making their way toward us, looking awestruck. Then she refocused on Violet. "Are you able to pop back into Mystica that easily, too?"

Sadness crossed over Violet's eyes. "Unfortunately, no," she said, clearly missing her old home. "My sisters and I are constantly using our magic to keep Avalon thriving. If we left, the island wouldn't be able to sustain everyone living here."

"Thank you," I said, reminded again how much Violet and her sisters had sacrificed to help us fight the demons on Earth.

"You're welcome," she said. "Although, what my

sisters and I are doing here isn't entirely unselfish. If the demons win the war on Earth, Mystica will be at risk of being invaded. We can't have that. So we're not just here for Earth, but for Mystica and all the other realms, too."

I assumed she was saying it for Jessica's benefit and not for mine, since she'd already told me as much during my orientation.

"You gave up your life in your home realm to help us fight against the demons," I said. "If that isn't unselfish, I don't know what is."

"You know a thing or two about that, don't you, Raven?" she said with a small smile.

"I guess so." I shrugged, since my journey here hadn't started out that way. It had started to help my mom. But sometime along the way, this fight against the demons had become my fight, too.

Especially since now, I was their only hope against Azazel.

The unicorns and wyverns got closer, until I could clearly see the humans on their backs. Leading the pack —one on a unicorn and the other on a wyvern—were two strong, beautiful, dark-skinned women, their long hair in tiny braids that flew out behind them.

They were the leaders of the academy, identical twin vampire princesses Darra and Tari from the Ward Kingdom in West Africa. Violet had told us about them during the tour of the manor house. Since they were in charge around here, they had the entire top floor of the house to themselves. Their quarters were private, so it was the one area we hadn't been allowed to see.

I recognized them immediately. Not because I'd met them before. But because I'd *seen* them before—in the video Thomas had shown me of Jacen's selection process he'd held in the Vale to find a bride. During the talent portion of the selection, they'd demonstrated their skills with fighting sticks. They were strong, fast, and lethal—no wonder they were the head trainers at the academy.

In the videos I'd seen from Jacen's selection, the twins had always looked uncomfortable in the gowns they'd worn in the palace. But now, riding on the backs of a wyvern and a unicorn as they charged back toward the academy, they looked completely in their element.

Once the group arrived in front of the manor house, the wyverns descended to deliver their humans to the ground.

Darra and Tari were the first to jump off the backs of their creatures. They each patted their creature's neck, as if thanking them for the ride, and stepped away. A second later, their creatures vanished into thin air.

Well, not technically into thin air. Thanks to what

Violet had just told me, I knew they had teleported back to Mystica.

The other students hopped off their creatures as well, doing the same thing Darra and Tari had done with placing a palm on their necks to thank them for the ride. A few seconds later, all the creatures were gone.

The princesses stepped forward to stand in front of us. "Welcome to Avalon Academy," said the one who had been riding the wyvern. She had strands of silver woven through her braids, while her sister had strands of gold. The students behind her were silent as she spoke. "I'm Tari."

"I'm Darra," said the one with gold strands who had ridden the unicorn. "We're the leaders of the academy, and will be overseeing your training."

"Now," Tari said, her sharp gaze focused on me. "What's the human whose form the Earth Angel used while she was masquerading as Princess Ana of the Seventh Kingdom doing at our door?"

Of course. They'd known "Princess Ana" from Jacen's selection process. And given what Tari had just said, Annika had come clean to them about what she'd done to masquerade as a vampire princess in the Vale.

"My name's Raven." I lifted my chin and held Tari's gaze. I'd been referred to as *the human* the entire time I was with Noah on his quest, and I hated it. "I'm here because I'll be training at the academy so I can enter the Angel Trials."

She narrowed her eyes in suspicion. "You were told what happens to the humans who go through the Angel Trials," she said, glancing at Violet as if this was a misunderstanding and it was the mage's fault. "Right?"

"I was." I didn't want to go through this conversation again. But I didn't have much of a choice. "Rosella, the vampire seer of the Haven, sent me here to enter the Trials. Because I'm a gifted human. My ability is my determination and stubbornness. If anyone can survive the Angel Trials, it's me."

"You're a dead girl walking." Tari raised her chin, not looking apologetic in the slightest. "You should turn around while you still can."

"Tari," Darra chided her sister. "You should be nicer. If Rosella sent Raven... maybe Raven *can* become a Nephilim."

"I doubt it," Tari said, still looking at me. "And even if there's a chance, why would you risk your life for us? The Earth Angel gave you memory potion and sent you back home to be with your family. Shouldn't you be back home with them instead of here, entering a trial that will kill you?"

The students standing behind them broke into murmurs of conversation amongst themselves. I couldn't catch much, but it sounded like they agreed with her.

"Two reasons." I spoke loudly, which got everyone to be quiet again. "Firstly, because of my gift, I sensed there was something wrong with my memories. And secondly, because the greater demon Azazel took my mom. He's taking gifted humans all across the country. He even took me for a few days, although I managed to escape."

"He took me too," Jessica chimed in, stepping forward so she was right beside me. "He had me turned into a vampire."

"Why would he do that?" Darra asked.

"I don't know," Jessica said. "I was rescued before he could finish with me."

"Rescued from where?"

"We'll fill you in on the details later," I said, since it didn't feel right to go into it with everyone listening. "The important part is that Azazel has blood bound himself with the Montgomery shifter pack. And the only way to sever the blood bond is to kill him."

"That's impossible." Horror dawned in Darra's eyes, her face turning ashen. "The only witch circle capable of such dark, ancient magic is the Foster circle. And the Foster witches all died during the Great War."

"Apparently not," I said. "Because they're still alive. And they're helping Azazel. I saw one of them myself."

"No," Tari said darkly. "We made sure they were dead. They can't be alive. It's not possible."

"It is," Jessica said. "My gift is that I can tell when someone's lying or telling the truth. And I promise you that right now, Raven's telling the truth."

Darra shook her head in shock, refocusing a moment later. "I believe you," she said. "Avalon wouldn't have accepted you onto the island if you came here to deceive us. You passed the simulation just as the rest of us did. You're one of us now. And here on Avalon, we trust each other."

"Good," I said. "Because Azazel needs to be stopped. I came here thinking I'd pass along the message and you'd send one of the Nephilim to take care of him. But clearly that's not happening. So now I'm going to enter the Angel Trials, become a Nephilim, and kill him myself."

"If you'd seen the way the humans before you died, you'd realize how foolish you're being by staying," Tari said. "But it's not my call to make."

"It's definitely not your call," Darra agreed with her sister, turning back to me. "I happen to think you're very brave. None of us would be on Avalon if it were truly impossible for humans to become Nephilim. If a seer sent you here, there's a possibility that you might be the first. We've been waiting for a sign, and I believe this is it. So I'll oversee your training myself."

"Wonderful." Violet brought her hands together and smiled down at everyone, as if she'd helped calm the waters between all of us instead of just standing there watching. "Now, to remind everyone, the welcome banquet for the new arrivals starts at nightfall. Don't be late." She gave another serene smile, and disappeared into thin air.

I'd never get used to the strangeness of seeing someone teleport.

"You heard her," Tari said to the crowd. Everyone in it was mostly looking at me like I was a cobra about to attack. Which was amusing, since I was the human and they were the powerful supernaturals. "It's time to clean up and get ready for dinner."

Once inside, Tari and Darra excused themselves to their top floor suite, although Darra assured me she'd see me at sunrise tomorrow to start training. I wasn't sure how I was supposed to wake up given that there were no clocks or watches on the island, but she was gone before I could ask. Hopefully one of the other students would clue me in. But when I looked around, they were already hurrying up the steps to their quarters.

I felt like a lost new girl as I stood there with Jessica, both of us unsure how to go about integrating ourselves with the others. This was a far cry from the bunker, where everyone had gone out of the way to make me feel welcome on my first day. I guessed there was a time crunch, since we had a limited amount of time to get ready. But I thought they would have made a bit more of an effort.

Luckily, three girls approached us. They all wore their hair in ponytails so high that it looked like they'd just come back from cheer practice. And were they wearing push up bras under their training uniforms?

They formed a circle around Jessica, leaving me standing on the outside.

"Hi!" The girl in the center—the blonde one—beamed. "I'm Samantha. This is Adriana and Ellen." She motioned first to the brunette on her left, and then the black haired girl on her right.

"Jessica," Jessica introduced herself, shaking Samantha's hand.

"And I'm Raven," I said, edging myself back into the circle. The dark haired girl—Ellen—gave me a nasty side eye and angled herself away from me.

Samantha glanced at me before focusing back on Jessica. "Wanna come get ready with us in our quarters?" she asked. "Since it's your first banquet, we can help you figure out what to wear."

"Thanks." Jessica managed a small smile, although she shifted in place, looking uncomfortable. "But I was going to get ready with Raven in the human quarters."

"Before Avalon, I was the fashion advisor to the princesses in the Tower," Adriana said in what sounded like a Spanish accent, sticking her nose up in the air. She eyed up Jessica's simple jeans and t-shirt, clearly assuming Jessica was clueless with fashion. "I know my stuff. You want to get ready with us—trust me."

"And there's no point getting close to the humans." Ellen flipped her long ponytail over her shoulder, purposefully swinging it into my face. "They all die after drinking from the Grail, anyway."

"Hey." I swatted Ellen's hair away and pushed past her, forcing my way into the circle. She must not have expected it, because even though vampires were *way* stronger than humans, I was able to get through. "I'm not going to die." I stared at each one of them, forcing them to finally look at me. "In case you missed what I said out there, I'm not just any human. I'm gifted. My gift is determination. And I'm determined to live."

For a moment, I thought I'd gotten through to them.

Then Samantha laughed.

"The others humans who trained here thought they were special, too." She rolled her eyes, like the thought of a unique human was ridiculous. "But once you enter the Angel Trials you're a dead girl walking, just like the rest of them."

Jessica curled her hands into fists, looking like she wanted to rip the perky blonde ponytail right off the Samantha's head. "Tell her how you really feel," she said, sarcasm dripping from her tone.

Samantha straightened and zoned in on me, her eyes

suddenly serious. "I think you're an egotistical human brat who's used to getting your way, and it's going to get you killed," she said, so intensely that she sounded like a robot. "Plus, you're the only girl at the academy who's prettier than I am. I don't want you taking any of *my* guys."

Her sidekicks looked at her like she'd lost her mind.

Then her eyes widened in shock, and she covered her mouth with her hands. "Omigosh," she said, dropping her hands back down and staring at me in horror. "I didn't mean to say that." She glanced at her friends, as if begging them to believe her. "It just came out. That was so unlike me. I don't know why I said that."

"She's telling the truth." Jessica tilted her head, confused.

I looked back and forth between Samantha and Jessica, putting the pieces together. "I think you just figured out how becoming a vampire heightened your gift," I said to Jessica. "You can force people to tell the truth."

A mischievous smile crossed my friend's face. "That'll come in handy," she said, and I nodded, agreeing with her.

"By the way," I said, turning back to Samantha. "I'm imprinted on a wolf shifter. Noah, from the Vale. I came here with him, and he's getting settled into his place here now. So there's no need to worry about me 'taking any of *your* guys.'" I couldn't help but chuckle as I said the final part. Because how many guys did Samantha think she "had?"

"Whatever." She flipped her blonde ponytail over her shoulder and scurried out of there. Her friends gave us one final glance—looking at Jessica like she was the Devil reincarnated—and followed behind.

Jessica and I were the only ones left in the grand foyer now that everyone else had gone to their quarters to get ready.

"Well," I said, glancing up at where the three vampire mean girls had disappeared. "That was interesting."

"It was," she agreed, still looking stunned from the discovery. I understood why—there was power in the truth. If Jessica could force the truth from people, it could seriously come in handy.

"Let's get ready in my quarters," I said, leading the way up the grand staircase. "And while we're getting ready, we can test out this heightened ability of yours to see how it works."

## RAVEN

*O*ur magical wardrobes supplied us with complete outfits for the banquet. Cocktail dresses, shoes, jewelry—the works. The heels were surprisingly comfortable. I guessed it was magic.

It had been a bit awkward accompanying Jessica into the female vampire quarters so she could grab her outfit to get ready in my room, but we managed. From the scared way everyone stared at Jessica, I had no doubt that Samantha had already filled them in on her ability. But we had each other, and that was all that mattered.

Darra had come to get us to make sure we wouldn't be late, which was nice of her. I was glad she was going to be my trainer.

Now I was standing in a sitting room outside of the banquet hall with Noah, Jessica, and Thomas. It was the first time I'd seen Noah dressed up. He wasn't in a full-blown suit like Thomas, but he was in nice pants and a button down top. He pulled it off well, except I could tell from the way he kept fidgeting with the sleeves that he felt far more comfortable in his typical jeans and t-shirt.

Iris—the third mage sister we hadn't met earlier—was there with us too. She had strawberry blonde hair, and was wearing a green medieval gown similar in style to what her sisters wore. The gown matched her emerald eyes. She was the event coordinator of Avalon, and had put together the banquet. She had a much warmer disposition than her two sisters.

As we waited for Bella, the four of us caught each other up on what had happened to us while we'd been apart. Noah's story made me tear up a bit. I was proud of him for accepting the position of alpha of the Southern Vale pack here on Avalon. He'd make a great leader. And I told him just that.

He was still wary about my decision to enter the Angel Trials, but he knew me well enough not to try to force me to change my mind. Because really, the more someone told me *not* to do something, the more determined I got to do it.

Finally, Bella rushed into the sitting room. She was wearing a skintight, short leather dress, and stiletto boots that went all the way up to her thighs.

If her goal was to get the attention of every single male on Avalon—and even the taken ones—she was definitely going to succeed.

"Glad to see the party didn't start without me," she said, strutting across the room to take a seat in one of the armchairs. "I don't know how you all manage to get places on time without watches."

"I'm on it," Thomas said. "Camelia has a shipment of watches arriving tomorrow. Enough for everyone on Avalon. I'll have them working and ready by tomorrow night."

"Impressive," Iris said. "We're glad to have you here." She walked to the front of the room, facing us. "Now that you're all here, it's time to formally introduce you to the citizens of Avalon," she said. "I'll introduce you one by one, saying your name, species, and where you're from. Then you'll take a seat at the head table with the Earth Angel, Jacen, and my sisters. But first, I need everyone wearing a cloaking ring to hand it over."

"Why?" Bella held her ring closer, looking instantly suspicious.

"On Avalon, you're safe from any danger," she said with a smile. "Etiquette here is the same as it is on Earth. It's impolite to wear cloaking rings when you're not out on a mission. We're here tonight to break bread—well, mana—and introduce you to everyone. How are they supposed to trust and accept you when you're cloaking your scents from them?"

"A valid point." Thomas—the first to understand everything regarding etiquette—removed his ring and handed it to Iris.

Noah followed suit, and finally Bella. Jessica didn't have a cloaking ring, since she'd been turned so recently. So I was the only one left.

"I know Avalon's safe," I started. "But won't it be dangerous to let out my human scent around vampires and shifters?" As much as I trusted Noah, Jessica, and Thomas, I had no reason to think the other vampires and shifters in the banquet hall wouldn't get a whiff of my human scent and decide they preferred to have me for dinner instead of the mana and Holy Water.

"The mana and Holy Water dull the natural cravings of vampires and shifters," Iris said. "They won't attack. And even if one of them did, they wouldn't get far before one of the other powerful supernaturals in the room—like my sisters or myself—intervened. They wouldn't be able to touch you."

"I'd rip them to shreds before they got close to you," Noah added casually.

"It's true," Jessica said. "You have nothing to worry about."

It made sense, and I *did* trust them—even before

Jessica used her gift to confirm it. So I removed my cloaking ring and added it to the pile on Iris's palm.

A moment later, all four of the rings exploded into a ball of green flames. It was so hot that I could feel the warmth against my face. The flames died down until they were gone—as were our rings.

Bella crossed her arms and glared at Iris. "Why did you *incinerate* our rings?" she snarled, looking like she was ready to pounce.

I didn't blame her. Sage had paid a *lot* for my ring. It wasn't exactly a disposable piece of jewelry.

"Relax." Iris laughed and brushed her hands off, even though there was no trace of ash on her palms. "I didn't incinerate anything. I used the same magic we use to send fire messages to deliver your rings back to your wardrobes. They'll be there when you return to your quarters tonight. It's the safest place for them, since the wardrobes are spelled so only their owners can open them."

"Oh." Bella instantly relaxed. "That makes sense. Thanks."

"No problem," she said. "Now, do you have any more questions?"

"When we enter the banquet hall, do we have to say anything?" Noah asked.

"No," Iris said. "Everyone will clap, and you'll sit

down. Once all of you are seated, the meal will be served. It'll be easy."

None of us had any more questions, which she seemed pleased about. I was also pleased, because I hadn't eaten much during my orientation. I'd been too shocked about the revelation that no one had yet to pass the Angel Trials. Now the hunger had caught up with me, and I was starving.

"You all look wonderful." Iris lifted her skirts, shot us an excited smile, and headed to the door. "Now please follow me to the banquet hall, and I'll get you introduced to the citizens of Avalon."

## RAVEN

$T$homas, Jessica, Bella, and Noah went first, in that order.

I hadn't been able to peek into the room yet, but it sounded like it was going well. Just as Iris had said it would. But I'd never been the type of person that enjoyed being in front of crowds, so butterflies were flapping in my stomach like crazy at the anticipation of going next.

The clapping died down, which I assumed meant Noah had been seated.

"You're up," Iris's assistant—a young witch named Natalie said.

"All right." I adjusted the straps of my dress, took a deep breath, and walked into the huge, high-ceilinged room.

The wooden furniture was so heavy and ornate that I felt like I'd stepped back in time. There were four long rows of tables set for royalty, with candlesticks, flowers, covered silver platters of what I assumed was filled with mana, and pitchers of Holy Water spread out in the centers. There were also bottles of wine—both white and red.

People in big chairs sat in front of each place setting. At the far left table I recognized the princesses Darra and Tari, along with some of the students from the academy, including Samantha and her cronies. Samantha watched me with the smuggest look ever. I wanted to wipe it right off her face. But my mood lightened when I saw Leia and the rougarou pack at the other side of the room. Leia even gave me a small nod of encouragement.

We'd come a long way since they'd attacked us and dragged us into their bar in New Orleans.

On the closest platform, perpendicular to the four long tables, Annika, Jacen, the mages, Noah, Thomas, Jessica, and Bella sat at a table facing the crowd. Annika looked worlds away from the depressed girl I'd met in her quarters. Wearing a brilliant gold dress that matched her eyes, makeup, and a regal up do in her hair, she appeared confident and poised. Like a true leader. No one would have been able to guess how much despair she'd been in a few hours earlier.

Iris was the only one standing. She motioned to the empty seat next to Noah and nodded for me to come forward.

"Lastly, this is Raven Danvers," she said, facing the crowd and projecting loudly enough to be heard in the back of the room. "A gifted human from Venice Beach, California."

No one clapped, and my stomach instantly felt like it dropped to my feet.

The shocked, wide eyes and open mouths staring back at me made it clear that they hadn't been prepared for the fact that a human was staying on Avalon. There were a few murmurs and shifting seats, but for the most part, everyone was quiet.

I'd been so worried that one of them would try to turn me into a snack that I hadn't stopped to think that they might not want me there.

I walked over to my seat, and for the first time in my life, I understood what people meant when they called silence "heavy." Because every step I took as the citizens of Avalon watched me like I didn't belong there felt like trudging through quicksand.

When I reached my seat, I didn't sit down. Instead, I placed my hand on the back of it and faced the crowd.

I hated that they'd clapped for everyone else, but not for me. I deserved better than that. I was also getting sick of explaining my existence here to everyone. So I might as well do it now, when I had the attention of everyone on the island. Then I could move on and be done with it.

"You all think I'm going to die," I said with a small laugh. "Don't you?"

"Sit down," Iris murmured from where she stood nearby. From the concerned way she was looking at me from the side of her eyes, she clearly thought I was about to lose it.

But the people at the long tables started nodding and answering my question, confirming that yes, they *did* think I was going to die. A few of them said I should go back home. That I wasn't safe on Avalon.

The more that they spoke, the more others felt comfortable chiming in, too.

"You're all wrong." I stood straighter and gazed down at them, shutting them up. "Like Iris said, I'm a *gifted* human. My gift is determination and stubbornness. The vampire seer Rosella sent me here so I can enter the Angel Trials and become a Nephilim. So that's what I'm going to do."

I scanned the crowd to see their reactions. Some

people were starting to nod in agreement, but not everyone looked convinced.

I wanted to convince them. So I continued, "The lives of people I love depend on me succeeding. The future of the world depends on me succeeding. Without Nephilim, you have no hope in beating the demons. So you better support me. Because right now, I'm the only chance you have. Especially since I'm determined to enter the Angel Trials and survive."

I stared out at them, daring them to contradict me. They didn't. Because what I'd said was true, and they all knew it.

Then, one person stood and started to clap. Darra. I could tell her apart from Tari because she had gold woven into her braids and Tari had silver. Her belief in me sent confidence shooting through my chest.

Another person stood and started clapping, then a few more, and then a few more, until the entire room exploded into applause. Even Samantha and her cronies were standing. Probably because they didn't want to be ostracized by remaining seated, but oh well. I'd take the win.

Heat rushed to my cheeks. I wasn't sure what else to say from there, so I sat down in my seat.

Noah leaned closer to me and gave me an encouraging smile. "You did great," he said. "I'd say they love you as much as I do, but that's impossible, since no one can ever love you as much as I do."

I totally would have kissed him right there if every citizen of Avalon wasn't watching. Instead, I took his hand under the table and held it in mine. Warmth and love poured through my body the moment our skin connected.

Ever since imprinting on Noah, I never ceased to be amazed about how much emotion could be conveyed with a single touch.

Jacen stood from his seat in the center of the table. Everyone quieted, and all eyes went to him. "Thank you, Raven," he said, giving me a respectful nod before returning his attention to the crowd. "The Earth Angel and I fully support Raven's decision to enter the Angel Trials, and we're glad to see you supporting her, too. Now, with that out of the way—let's eat."

He sat back down, and Iris joined her sisters on the other side of our table. Once everyone in the room was seated, Annika removed the lid from the platter in front of her. As expected, it was full of mana.

That was apparently the cue people needed to remove the lids from the platters closest to them, too.

Holy Water and wine were poured, bread—well, mana—was broken, and everyone talked excitedly amongst themselves. The entirety of the banquet hall was aglow in warm candlelight from the chandeliers overhead. Iris sure did know how to host a feast.

The mana tasted like pizza, and it was the best pizza I'd ever tasted. I would have paired it with red wine, but I needed to be up early for my first day of training tomorrow morning. Sunrise. Ugh. Best to stick with Holy Water tonight.

"Earlier, I was worried when you told me you were entering the Angel Trials," Noah said once we'd started slowing down on our food. "I still *am* worried. But I hope you know that I know you have to do this. And that I'd never stop you. Because what you said about you being our best chance at beating the demons is right. And I'm going to do everything I can to support you and help you succeed."

"You better," Thomas said, his eyes dark as he looked at Noah and me. Apart from politely answering a few of Jacen's questions about the technology he planned on bringing to Avalon, Thomas had been quiet for the majority of the meal. This was the most emotion I'd seen from him since we'd arrived. "You're our only chance to kill Azazel and free Sage. We're counting on you not to mess this up."

Way for him to put on the pressure... as if I wasn't feeling it already.

"By 'mess this up,' you mean you're counting on me not to die?" I asked.

"Yes," he said. "Exactly."

"Don't worry." I wished I could channel the surge of confidence I'd felt when I was trying to convince the entire banquet hall to believe in me. "I'm going to do my best. I swear it."

He nodded, and that was that.

But despite what I'd said to the crowd, I couldn't help wondering—was my best going to be good enough?

## KARA

*T*he past day had flown by in a blur.

After Harry had killed the supernatural that had been waiting for us at the riverbank, I'd led him and my twin brother Keith through the woods toward the nearest small town.

Harry had robbed the first empty house we'd come across. A cabin that looked to be a summer home. There wasn't much cash inside, but there were clothes we could wear instead of the white outfits given to us at the Haven. The clothes were a bit big for Keith and me, but with a bit of digging, we found some that worked.

More importantly, there was a truck. The people who owned the cabin were apparently super trusting— or we were just in a safe area—because they'd left the keys to the truck in the garage. Which made it easy for Harry to steal.

I hadn't wanted him to steal. I'd asked him not to. But then he'd pointed out that we needed a car. It wouldn't be long until the supernaturals from the Vale wondered where we were and found the body we'd left behind. If we stayed on foot, they'd smell our trail. Then we'd be right back where we started. Except we'd be in big trouble, since Harry had killed one of their men, and I'd helped us escape.

This truck would save our lives. So I guessed I was okay with Harry stealing it.

We made a few stops in random places along the road to town, including places not on the way. There, we got out and walked around for a few minutes. Harry claimed if we left our scent in a bunch of random places, it would throw off any supernatural trackers.

Eventually, Harry found a local bar a few towns away. There, he bet on games of darts and pool, using his gift of perfect aim to win every time. No one paid much attention to "his kids"— Keith and me—sitting in a nearby booth. They were too amazed by Harry's ability to win every game.

Once we had enough cash, we hit the road again.

I wanted Harry to drive us to the nearest police station. But what were we going to tell them? That we'd been kidnapped by a demon, held in a bunker, teleported by witches to India, teleported again to a hidden vampire kingdom in the Canadian Rockies, and then denied entrance to a mystical hidden island called Avalon?

No one would believe us. Worse, Harry thought the authorities would assume *he'd* kidnapped my brother and me.

He worried the entire way to the nearest city, Banff. Especially because without identification, it was going to be impossible for us to get back to the US. He ultimately decided we needed to have our families come to us and bring us our birth certificates and stuff to get us back home.

He stopped at a convenience store to buy one of those disposable phones, but he hadn't used it yet. Because he still wasn't sure what he should say to our families. If we told them the truth and the authorities made our story public, the supernaturals would easily find us again. Then we'd be right back where we'd started.

"There needs to be a witness protection program for humans," Harry muttered. He was on edge, continuously looking out for cops even though the owners of the truck hadn't been to their cabin in months and wouldn't know to report their truck as stolen. "Something to get us back to our normal lives after what we went through."

"Maybe we should have gone back to the Vale," Keith finally said. "They might have helped us get in touch with our families."

"They wouldn't have." Harry glared at him through the rearview mirror. He'd insisted we both sit in the back, even though we were twelve and one of us could have sat in front. But my brother and I had wanted to sit with each other, so we hadn't pushed it. "They're monsters—all of them. Abominations. You heard what Mary said at the Haven. She wanted to turn us into vampires. Immortal, soulless creatures doomed to Hell. She made it sound like it was our choice, but she was lying. If we'd stayed there—at either the Haven or the Vale—we would have been at their mercy. You kids were lucky you were with me at that riverbank so I could get us out of there."

I stared out the window at the passing mountains, not saying anything for a few seconds. Because I'd learned about creatures like these in Sunday school. Witches, vampires, shifters... they were all monsters. Just as bad as the demons. They might have acted nice to us, but that was all it was. An act.

Since the day Keith and I had been kidnapped, we'd been praying for help. In the bunker together, we'd prayed every night before bed. When we'd first learned about the Earth Angel on Avalon, we thought she was the answer to our prayers. That was why we'd agreed to go to Avalon in the first place. Surely an *angel* would help us.

But Avalon had denied us.

Maybe Harry helping us escape was the true answer to our prayers.

I reminded my brother as much, and he agreed.

"You kids still believe in God after everything we've been through?" Harry asked.

"Of course." I reached for the cross necklace I always wore. The demons had taken it away from me in the bunker, but the witches had returned it to me in the Haven. "Don't you?"

"I don't know what I believe anymore." He turned up the volume of the stereo, not leaving it up for discussion. The car only had one of those ancient radios in it, so there was more static than actual music.

None of us spoke for a few minutes.

"When will we get to see our parents?" I eventually asked.

"Soon, kid," he said. "Soon."

Once we arrived in Banff, Harry drove us to a motel near the airport. It was one of those grungy motels that had a lit up neon sign saying, "vacancy" near the side of the road. If it hadn't been for the sign, I would have thought it was abandoned.

"Not the nicest place ever," he said as he pulled into a spot. "But hopefully they won't care that we don't have IDs."

The person working the check in counter *did* ask for ID, but he was willing to forget about it when Harry handed him an extra wad of cash.

Harry got our key, and we walked silently to the room. It had worn carpeting, stains on the beds, and smelled like mothballs.

I wished we were home and not here.

"Are you kids cool with sharing a bed?" Harry asked, since there were only two beds in the room.

"Sure," Keith said. "I don't sleep much, anyway."

That was my twin's gift. He only needed about two hours of sleep each night. My parents had gotten him checked out by so many doctors, but he had no abnormal brain activity, so none of them could figure out the cause. Eventually my parents chalked it up to a blessing from God and left it at that.

I was just opening the nightstand drawer to see if there was a Bible inside when two people appeared in the room. A man in ripped jeans and a leather jacket, and a pale woman with jet-black hair that flowed to her waist.

Supernaturals. They'd found us. I didn't know how, since we'd taken so much care to cover our tracks, but they were here.

The man moved to Harry in a blur and cuffed his hands behind his back.

I screamed and ran to the door. But the woman blocked my path, grabbing me.

I saw the man holding onto Harry and my brother, then the dingy motel room disappeared, and I was sucked into darkness.

## KARA

*I* appeared in a big living room a second later. The woman was still holding onto my arm. The man appeared nearby, holding onto my brother and Harry. There were two other men standing by the door, guarding it. One of them was younger and meaner looking. The other appeared to be about my dad's age, and I could have sworn he looked at me with a flash of pity. It was replaced by a blank expression a moment later.

There were leather sofas in the room, and a big window looking out to the mountains. Everything in the room was dark brown, like a cabin. I quickly used my gift to pinpoint our location.

Los Angeles, California. Right in the Hollywood Hills.

"I want them turned," the leather-clad man who had

taken Harry and Keith said to the nicer looking man standing by the door.

"I can turn the man," he said. "But the children are too young. They won't survive it."

"Derrick," the leather-clad man said the name with little patience in his tone. "Turn them. Now."

"Turn us into what?" I asked, panic rising in my throat. Because I had a dreadful feeling he meant turned into a vampire. Like what had happened to Jessica.

He ignored me. I looked around at everyone else in the room—Derrick, the woman by my side, and the other guard at the door—but they ignored me, too.

Struggle flashed in Derrick's eyes, but he walked toward Harry anyway.

Harry tried to run, but the leather clad man held him by both arms. My brother hurried to my side, trembling with fear. The woman let go of my arm, apparently not deeming me a threat. But she remained close to my side.

"Wait," the leather clad man said.

Derrick stopped walking. "Yes, Azazel?" he asked.

Azazel. This was the greater demon Raven had told us about. The one who was in charge of bringing us to the bunker.

I curled my hands into fists. I hated Azazel with every fiber of my being.

I'd prayed for an angel to save me, but had been delivered into the hands of a demon.

Maybe Harry was right to doubt God was listening to us.

"I want to find out what their gifts are first," Azazel said. "I already know Harry's gift—he was on high alert at the bunker because of it. But I don't know the kids'. It would be impulsive to put them at risk if their gifts might be useful."

Derrick nodded, clasped his hands behind his back, and waited.

"Hold him down," Azazel instructed, motioning to Harry. "Make sure he doesn't try to run. Not that he'd get far. But we don't want to cause a commotion when it isn't necessary."

Derrick did as instructed and took over the job of holding down Harry. He was like a zombie, mindlessly obeying Azazel's every command.

With Harry off his hands, Azazel walked closer to my brother and me, kneeled down to be at our level, and smiled.

The smile was obviously fake. It sent chills up my arms.

"What are your gifts?" he asked, looking back and forth between the two of us. "And I recommend you get out with it. Otherwise we'll have to do this the hard way. That would be fun for me. But not for you."

I gulped, not liking how that sounded. "I have a perfect sense of direction," I said, since what harm would it do to be honest with him?

"Interesting." He tilted his head. "Is that all?" The wicked gleam in his eyes warned me to be truthful with him.

"I always know where I am," I said. "I know the location of other places, too, and how to get to them. Like a GPS inside my head."

"Where are we now?" he asked.

"Hollywood Hills, California." I continued on to give him the exact coordinates, in case he doubted me.

"Fascinating." He grinned and clapped a few times, the hollow sound echoing through the room. "And how far are we from… I don't know. Las Vegas?"

The answer popped into my head instantly, just like when typing it into Google Maps. "Las Vegas is 277 miles away from here," I said. "You'd take I-15 north to get there."

His smile widened. "Impressive," he said. "Now, can you tell me the location of an island called Avalon?"

The island where the Earth Angel lived with her army. Azazel wanted to go there.

He couldn't go there. I had a dreadful feeling that if he did, all hope would be lost.

I thought about Avalon, and a bunch of possible locations popped into my mind. Most weren't islands. And I was positive that none of them were the Avalon he was looking for.

The Avalon that had rejected me.

"Do you mean the town on Santa Catalina Island in California?" I asked.

"No." His grin disappeared. "Avalon is the name of the island. Not a city on an island."

I searched again. Nothing. Even if I *wanted* to locate Avalon, I couldn't do it.

"There's a test to try to get to Avalon," I said the only thing that came to my mind. The only thing that might save us. "A simulation. You get on boats to take it. I can tell you where the start of the simulation is."

"I know all about King Arthur's simulation." Azazel's eyes were scarily calm. "We all know I won't pass it. No point in pretending I have a chance. I need the exact location of the island."

"I can't find it." Terror brewed in my stomach, since I knew it wasn't what he wanted to hear. "I'm trying. But I can't find it."

"It's hidden." He snarled. "Apparently even from you. Well, it's hidden from you while you're still human." He turned his focus to my brother, apparently not interested in me anymore. "What's your gift?" he asked Keith.

My brother trembled and stepped toward me. He looked at me with big, frightened brown eyes that I had a feeling matched my own, and I nodded at him to go on.

I was scared of what Azazel might do to us if we didn't tell him what he wanted.

"I don't need much sleep," Keith said. "Maybe two hours a night, at most."

"Hmm," Azazel said, his gaze traveling back to me. "How old are you?"

"Twelve," I answered. "We're twins."

"Perfect." The glint returned to his eyes, and he stood up, facing Derrick again. "Turn Harry and the boy. I'll see how the boy fares, and then I'll decide what to do with his sister."

"Here?" Derrick glanced at me and then around the fancy living room, his eyes wide in alarm.

"Good point." Azazel looked at Derrick in approval. "I like this room and don't want to mess up the furniture. Do it in the pool house. No one lives there anymore. It's the perfect place for our experiments."

Derrick and the other man grabbed Harry and my brother and dragged them out of the room.

I screamed my brother's name and tried to run after

him, but the dark-haired lady held me back. I tried to fight her, but she was stronger than me. So I kept repeating my brother's name, begging for him not to be taken away from me, tears streaming down my face as the doors slammed shut behind him.

He was gone. All was silent except for my cries.

And I was left in this awful room with the scary lady and Azazel.

*I* sat in the bed of my room in the Montgomery compound, watching reruns of an old show on television. I'd eventually drift off to sleep with the show still on and wake up at sunset when Lavinia knocked on the door with my breakfast of blood and complacent potion, like I did every morning.

That was my life since getting here. Drinking blood to stay alive, getting dosed with complacent potion, and watching television. I'd tried practicing yoga—an activity I'd always loved—but it did nothing to calm my thoughts. Only mindless television was doing that, and barely.

I'd also tried using what little tools were available to me—mainly ripped pages from books and bits of blood I was able to resist drinking from my meals—to create a tarot deck of my own. Then I could do a reading and see how Raven was doing. But the deck was worthless.

My ability apparently only worked when handling a *real* deck. And I was only allowed access to one of those when Azazel needed a reading from me. Even then, he commanded what reading I'd do. And thanks to the complacent potion, I had to follow his orders.

I was finally drifting to sleep when there was a knock on the door, startling me awake.

A glance at the clock showed it was just past 1:00 pm. The middle of the night for supernaturals, because of their nocturnal schedule. No one ever came to my room at this time.

I inhaled, breathing in the scent of sickly sweet syrup. Lavinia.

I reached for the remote and turned off the TV. "Come in," I said, sitting up in bed. I tried to look calm, not wanting to give her the satisfaction of knowing she'd startled me.

She threw the door open and studied me, looking unimpressed as always. "Get up," she said. "Azazel wants you in the main house."

My heart jumped into my throat. I'd been kept prisoner in this room since being brought to the Montgomery compound. Whatever Azazel needed me for was obviously important.

Hopefully nothing bad had happened to Raven.

"Did you hear me?" Lavinia glared at me like I was an imbecile. "Azazel needs you. Now. So get out of bed and follow me. His Grace doesn't like to be kept waiting."

Lavinia led me from my room to the main house across the lawn. She'd brought me an umbrella, so the mid-day sun wouldn't burn me.

Heaven forbid anything might hurt their treasured prophetess.

It was my first time being outside since... well, I'd lost track of how many days it had been since Azazel had taken me from the apartment. It felt like it had been weeks.

Looking around, the Montgomery compound seemed to be a grouping of luxury houses at the top of the Hollywood Hills. It would have been pretty, if the people who lived there weren't monsters. No one milled about right now except for us, since they were all asleep.

Once in the main house, Lavinia pushed open double doors leading to a huge living room. There were three other people inside. Azazel, a male vampire who looked around my age, and a young girl who was curled into ball on the couch crying. I immediately recognized her from the bunker. And thankfully, from the smell of her, she was still human.

"Kara." I hurried toward her and wrapped her into a hug. The strong scent of her blood hit me with my first breath in, and my fangs ached inside my gums. A carnal part of me wanted to sink them into her neck and taste her young blood fresh from the vein. But I controlled myself. Kara needed me right now. And despite what I was now, I'd never hurt her—or anyone. "What happened to you?" I asked.

She shook her head and stared straight ahead, her eyes empty.

Whatever had happened to her since the last time I'd seen her had clearly traumatized her.

Seeing her like this only made me hate Azazel more. I kept one arm around her and let her burrow into my side, wanting her to know she wasn't alone.

"Skylar," Azazel said, stepping in front of where I sat with Kara. He had his annoying trademark grin that I always wanted to rip off his face. "Welcome to the main house. Would you like a cookie?" He motioned to a plate of them on the coffee table. Chocolate chip.

"I'm a vampire..." I reminded him, looking at him like he'd lost his mind.

"So what?"

"I survive on blood."

He threw back his head and laughed. "You mean you don't know?" he asked once he'd gotten control of himself. "Don't answer that—I can tell by your expression that you don't. Let me enlighten you. Vampires don't have to survive only on blood. You can eat food, too. So have a cookie. They're delicious." He reached for one and took a huge bite, smiling to prove his point.

I eyed up the cookies in question. After surviving only on liquid since being turned into a vampire, solid food *did* sound good. "Are they vegan?" I asked.

Sure, now I had to drink blood, which technically didn't make me a vegan anymore. But the reasons I became a vegan—to not support animal cruelty, and to protect the environment—still existed. And I'd continue to be the best vegan I could be, despite my condition.

"What is it with the strange diet requirements of people on Earth?" Azazel laughed again. "I see it everywhere here in LA. Vegan, gluten-free, keto, dairy-free, paleo, juicing. What ever happened to just enjoying plain old food?"

I didn't answer, since it seemed like he was only speaking to hear himself talk. I also didn't take a cookie.

"Why did you need to see me?" I asked.

"Skipping the pleasantries and getting straight to the point," he said, sitting in the armchair across from Kara and me. "I like it." He popped the rest of the cookie in his mouth, finishing it off and wiping the crumbs from the stubbly beard on his chin.

I stared at him, waiting for him to continue. The others in the room—Lavinia and the vampire—stood along the wall, not saying a word.

"I just tried to have Kara's brother turned into a vampire," Azazel started. "*Tried* being the key word. He rejected the venom and didn't survive the change."

Kara trembled at the mention of her brother, and I could smell the salty tears that streamed down her face. Poor Keith. I hadn't known him well, but he seemed like a sweet, innocent boy. My heart went out to him and his grieving sister. I pulled Kara closer to comfort her, even though nothing but time was going to dull her pain.

"Derrick over there says it's because the boy was too young to be turned." Azazel glanced at the other vampire in the room, who I assumed was Derrick. "I need Kara turned, and I need her to survive the transition. So it's time you do another tarot reading for me to find out when I'll be able to do that."

Lavinia walked over and dropped my tarot deck onto the coffee table in front of me. Thanks to the complacent potion I was being dosed with, I didn't have a choice if I wanted to do as Azazel asked or not. So I reached for the cards, shuffled, and pulled one from the deck.

The Empress.

A woman in a red gown stood in a blooming garden, her hands cradling her pregnant stomach. I knew this card well. It represented femininity, harmony, and fertility, amongst other things.

As had started happening with my heightened vampire gift, the image on the card disappeared, replaced by a scene playing out in front of me.

It was Kara, and she didn't appear to be much older than she was now. Maybe only a few months. She was holding her stomach as if in pain and running to a bathroom. The vision adjusted my view to protect her privacy, but I was able to see that once inside, there was blood spotting the inside of her underwear. As she looked around the bathroom to figure out what to do, the panic in her eyes made it clear what was happening. Her first period.

Once I understood what was going on, the vision disintegrated and I was once again staring at the regular Empress card.

"Well?" Azazel leaned forward and rested his elbows on his knees. "What did you see?"

I tried pressing my lips together to fight against the complacent potion. I didn't *want* to answer his question. Everything I told him worked directly against Raven.

Rage coursed through my veins as I stared back at

him. But as always, the potion won, forcing the words out of my mouth without my consent.

"You have to wait until Kara gets her first period to turn her," I said. "If you try before then, she'll reject the venom and die."

"Period?" Azazel's eyebrows knit together in confusion.

"Monthly menstrual cycle," I clarified.

"Ah." Understanding flashed in his eyes. "Her first moon bleed. When will that occur?"

Kara pulled away from me and stared up at me, her watery eyes frightened and betrayed.

I didn't blame her. I'd hate myself if I were her, too.

I needed to get free from here. I didn't know how to do it, but I refused to be Azazel's slave forever.

"I can't be sure," I answered honestly. "But she didn't look much older than she does now. It could be a few months. Maybe a year. I don't think it'll be longer than that."

"Fantastic." Azazel brought his hands together, smiling again. "Lavinia—bring Kara to the guest house and get her settled into a room there. She'll be staying with us until her first moon bleed. And once she's turned…" He focused on Kara, his eyes narrowing in greed. "I can't wait to see how her gift heightens when she's a vampire."

*L*avinia left with Kara, leaving me alone with Azazel and Derrick.

"The tarot reading you gave me the other day allowed me to capture Kara, Keith, and Harry," Azazel said to me. "You've earned the privilege of being able to move freely around the compound. But if you purposefully keep anything from me again, that privilege will be revoked. Understand?"

"I understand." I nodded. "If we're finished, I'd like to return to my room now."

The less time I had to spend in Azazel's presence, the better. I was also disgusted at myself for what I'd just done. Right now, I needed sleep. I'd start exploring the compound at nightfall.

Derrick smiled at me in a way I could have sworn

was flirtatious. "Would you like me to walk you back?" he asked.

"I can get back myself." I squared my shoulders, not meeting his eyes. Because yes, Derrick was attractive. And he was my age—or at least he'd been my age when he was turned into a vampire. But I had no intention of getting involved with any of Azazel's supporters, no matter how good-looking they might be.

Azazel looked back and forth between Derrick and me, grinning. That stupid, arrogant grin. The one that immediately let me know he was amused or planning something. Probably both.

Finally, he focused on Derrick. "I'd try to hit that too, if I didn't find younger women the most appealing," he said, which made me bristle. Because sure, I wasn't in my twenties anymore, but I took care of my health. I hardly looked *old*. "Skylar," he continued, looking at me. "I command you to allow Derrick to walk you back to your room."

I pressed my lips together and dug my nails into my palms.

I needed this complacent potion out of my system. Unfortunately, that was going to be difficult, since I was being dosed twice a day by needle.

"You two have fun together," Azazel said, still grinning. "Now, if you'll excuse me. I need to find someone to clean up the mess in the pool house."

He flashed out, leaving Derrick and me alone together.

Derrick picked up the umbrella Lavinia had left behind and handed it to me. "You coming?" he asked, grabbing an umbrella of his own that he must have left by the entrance.

"I don't have much of a choice." I opened the door and stormed out of it before he could do it for me.

He walked beside me on the way out of the main house, not saying a word. Then, once we were halfway between the main house and the guest house, he stopped in his tracks.

"What are you doing?" I glared at him, since even though we were under umbrellas, the afternoon sun was still oppressive against my now sensitive skin.

"I wanted to talk to you," he said. "The demons could have been listening to us in the main house, and there are spells cast in the rooms of the guest house to listen in and make sure we're all behaving ourselves."

"We're?" I raised an eyebrow at his interesting choice of words. "You make yourself sound like a prisoner, too."

"You think I want to be here?" He looked at me like I'd lost my mind. His eyes were a startlingly beautiful shade of ice blue... and I immediately chided myself for staring into his eyes. "I'm on your side," he continued. "We're both vampires. We stick together."

"The only other vampires I've met are the ones who turned me," I said. "Dmitri and Natasha. I didn't see much of them, but they were definitely on the side of the demons."

"They're from the Carpathian Kingdom," he muttered, shaking his head. "They promised they'd given up their Foster witch connection. I guess they lied." He focused on me, his gaze intense. "But that's not important right now. What's important is that you know I'm under complacent potion, just like you. I was one of their test subjects to get the complacent potion working on vampires."

"What do you mean?" I asked.

He glanced around, as if paranoid someone might be listening in. But since it was the middle of the night for those on nocturnal schedules, the yard was empty. "Complacent potion is illegal," he said quickly. "Any witch caught brewing it will have her powers stripped. So most witches don't know how to make it anymore. The knowledge has been lost to most circles. But even when it used to be used millennia ago, it only worked on humans. This complacent potion that works on supernaturals is new. It was created by Lavinia and the other

Foster witches." His eyes darkened, and he continued, "To create it, they experimented. On me and my coven."

"Wow." I didn't expect to be rendered speechless on this walk back to my room, but now I was. "I'm sorry."

"I'm the only one left," he said. "That's why Azazel keeps me here. I'm a reminder about what he and the Foster witches can achieve while they're working together. I'm not on his side. But I'm pretending to be."

"You want to gain his trust," I realized.

"Exactly," he said, and just like that, a connection forged between us. "Complacent potion is difficult to make, which makes it rare. Azazel doesn't want to give it to us—he *has* to. So I want him to think I'm on his side, so he stops giving it to me. Once that happens, I'll escape."

"Azazel would never fall for that," I said. "Not after what he did to you and your coven."

"He's so egotistical that he might," Derrick said. "I've spent enough time with him by now that I'm starting to understand the way he thinks. He values self-preservation above all else. That's why he wanted to work with the alpha of the Montgomery pack—Flint. Azazel saw some of himself in Flint. But I'm getting off track, and we don't have much more time. There's always a way out of every situation, so my plan's at least worth a try.

And I want you as an ally. Your gift is impressive. We can do great things if we work together."

We were huddled so closely together under our umbrellas that anyone looking at us would probably assume we were lovers having an intimate conversation. Not that anyone was looking on. Derrick had made sure of that.

"Azazel has commanded that I only do tarot readings for him," I said. "So as long as I'm under complacent potion, I'm bound to comply to his order. And while maybe he'll eventually believe you're on his side, he'd never believe that about me. Trust me."

"Maybe," he said. "Maybe not. Either way, you're not confined to your room anymore. It might be worth it to venture out tomorrow and try making connections with the others at the compound. Not that there's much left of them to connect with anymore…"

"What do you mean by that?" I asked.

"If you want to find out, you should see for yourself tomorrow," he said with a knowing glint in his eyes. "But we've been standing here for long enough, and I don't want to test our luck. Allow me to escort you back to your room?"

He held out his elbow like a gentleman from one of those historical movies.

Since he was an immortal vampire, maybe he *had*

been one of those gentlemen at one point in his life. There was a lot I wanted to learn about him. But later— when we weren't trapped in the scorching sunlight. Because even through the umbrella, the sun burned.

And now that I was trapped in the Montgomery compound with nothing to do except a tarot reading for Azazel every few days, I had tons of free time.

"Thank you." I linked my arm into his, a newfound sense of power filling my veins at the thought of having some sort of plan. Sure, the plan wasn't much, but it was better than nothing. "And Derrick?," I said, prompting him to look over at me in curiosity. "I'm glad we had this chat."

"So you'll consider my offer?" he asked.

"Yes," I said with a small smile. "I most certainly will."

# RAVEN

The doors to my room slammed open, startling me out of a deep sleep.

I groaned and turned over to see who was there.

Darra stood at the foot of my bed, staring me down. She wore the black Avalon Academy training outfit, her hair was pulled up into a high ponytail, and she had a sword strapped to her belt.

She totally could have killed me in my sleep.

It was a good thing we were fighting on the same side.

I glanced at the window—I'd purposefully left the curtains open so the natural sunlight would wake me up. We weren't supposed to start training until sunrise. But it was still dark out. So why was Darra here?

My thoughts instantly went to the worst possible scenario.

"What happened?" I sat up quickly, fear rushing through my veins. "Is Noah okay?"

"Your future mate is fine," Darra said, her voice steady and calming. "But the sun is about to rise, and you're starting training *at* sunrise—not after it. So get out of bed, get dressed, and meet me in the dining hall."

She turned on her heel and left, not giving me time to ask any questions.

After freshening up in the bathroom—which I didn't have to share with anyone, since the bathrooms were also separated by species and gender—I got dressed as quickly as possible. The black training outfit was a one-piece pull up thing made of a comfortable, breathable, stretchy material. I felt like I was putting on a costume for a superhero movie. And the matching black sneakers were bouncy and comfortable. I pulled my hair up into a pony-tail, since obviously I'd need one today, and was ready.

Darra was the only other one in the dining hall when I arrived. She was sitting at the long table by herself with a plate of mana and glass of Holy Water. There was a matching place setting across from her. "Eat." She motioned to the food across from her. "You'll need the energy."

*That* was foreboding. So much for hoping I might be eased into my training.

I sat down and started to eat. The mana tasted like chocolate chip pancakes. Delicious.

"Where's everyone else?" I asked, looking around the otherwise empty room.

"They won't wake up until a bit later," she said. "You need an earlier start, since you have a lot to cover."

I sighed and finished up my breakfast. I was *not* a morning person. Luckily, the Holy Water was making me feel more awake and alert, like a strong cup of coffee.

Once I finished, Darra led me out to the back of the manor house. The first rays of sunlight were beginning to peek their way over the tallest hill in the background. Straight in front of us was a track and another large building—the gym. Violet had pointed the gym out to Jessica and me during our tour yesterday, but hadn't shown us the inside.

Looked like I was going to be seeing it now.

"Get on the track and run," she said, motioning to the oval track in front of us.

I groaned inwardly. I *hated* running. "For how long?" I asked.

"Until you can't run any further."

She sat down on the bleachers and made herself

comfortable. Right next to the bleachers was an old, stone well. Hopefully it functioned. Because I was definitely going to need water after this.

With Darra's eyes on me, I grudgingly stepped onto the track and started to run. At first it felt good, with my hair flying behind me and my sneakers padding along the track. It was like the mana and Holy Water had given me bonus energy. Call me crazy, but I could almost say I was *enjoying* running.

That didn't last for long.

First, my legs started to feel like lead weights. Then my chest hurt each time I took a breath. I felt like an out of water fish gasping for air, but each breath sent slicing pain into my lungs. Sweat dripped down from my hairline, and I wiped it away from my eyes so I could see. This was awful. I tried pushing through despite the pain, but then the stomach cramp hit. Sharp and jolting, it made me grab my side and forced me to stop running.

I would have collapsed on the spot if my body wasn't screaming at me to give it water. So I hobbled over to the well, where Darra had thankfully already reeled up a bucket of water.

I reached for the ladle inside and downed it, dipping it back in and drinking until I couldn't drink any more. Judging from the kick of energy it gave me, this was

Holy Water, just like all the other fresh water I'd had so far on Avalon.

"How did I do?" I asked Darra once I'd caught my breath enough to speak.

"Terribly." Her eyes were hard, and I could have sworn I saw a trace of worry in them. "You didn't even complete a mile."

"Was I at least close?"

"You were close to completing a mile." She nodded, as if giving me credit where it was due. "But one of your trials is to run a marathon."

"Oh." My heart sunk into my stomach. "How many miles are in a marathon?"

"Twenty-six point two."

"Crap." I stared at the track in defeat. Running for that long sounded impossible.

Completing a marathon had never been on my bucket list, and there was a good reason why. Gym had always been my least favorite class in middle school. Especially when we were forced to run around the field to warm up.

But I didn't come to Avalon to give up on the first morning of training. And regular humans on Earth ran marathons all the time. Athletic, strong, sporty humans, but humans nonetheless.

If they could train to run a marathon, then so could

I. Especially since I was a gifted human fueled by mana and Holy Water.

"So… how do I train to run a marathon?" I asked, trying to force excitement into my tone that I definitely didn't feel.

From the sharp look Darra gave me, she didn't buy it. But she continued anyway. "From your starting place—which is basically the very beginning—training to run a marathon will take anywhere from twelve to twenty weeks," she said.

"Oh." I smiled. "That's not as bad as I expected."

"What did you expect?"

"I don't know." I shrugged. "A year?"

"God help us if it takes a year," she said, and I felt the full pressure of her words on my chest. Because we really *would* need some kind of Heavenly intervention if no humans were able to pass the Angel Trials.

The reminder of why it was so important that I do this gave me a wave of energy. Well, that plus the Holy Water I was still sipping on from the ladle.

"You'll be running three to five times a week," she said. "You'll start from your base point, which we just found out was one mile. You'll gradually increase the amount you're running each time, until you're able to do the full marathon."

"Okay." I nodded, since that didn't sound *too* bad. "I

can do that. And I'll be running five times a week. Not three."

"That's what I like to hear." Darra looked pleased for the first time since she'd sent me out onto the track. "Now, follow me to the gym," she said. "It's time for interval training."

*I*. Hated. Interval training.

It was similar to the type of training I had to do in the bunker, which meant it was *torture*. Each session was only twenty-eight minutes long, which didn't sound bad when Darra first told me. It was broken up into sections of seven minutes of going all out, with one minute to rest in between. It was ridiculously hard, and I was a sweaty, disgusting mess once I finished.

If you could even call what I did "finishing." Darra had told me that the gym was there specifically for humans doing training, so luckily there was no one else in there but the two of us. Because I struggled hard.

The worst were the burpees—a full body exercise

that Darra promised would help me gain strength and endurance. She'd asked me to do ten of them.

I could barely manage three in a row before needing a break. But somehow, I huffed and puffed my way through all ten burpees, with lots of breaks in between. It wasn't pretty. Especially when they popped up in the workout again. They were harder the second time.

Then there were the push-ups. Just like in the bunker, I still couldn't do a push-up. Darra had me do them on my knees to build up my arm strength so I'd eventually be able to do them for real. But I even struggled with those, needing breaks in between.

The easiest were the squats. At least I could get through those without feeling like I was going to keel over and die.

Until Darra told me to do *jump* squats. Ugh. They were awful.

The entire session was awful. Even though the intervals were only seven minutes, each one felt like an eternity. An eternity of me huffing, puffing, sweating, feeling like my muscles were jelly, and barely being able to breathe. At least I had the minute between each interval to somewhat catch my breath and drink some Holy Water. I couldn't have gotten through the exercises without it.

I didn't even want to think about how sore I'd be tomorrow.

Finally, Darra led me through the cool down, and I collapsed onto the mat in a heap. "That was terrible." I sneaked a peek at her, embarrassed by my performance.

From her crossed arms and closed, pursed lips, she clearly agreed with me.

"You'll improve," she said. "Interval training is a fantastic way to build both muscle and endurance. Many of the humans who trained here started off worse than you did. But they all improved quickly—especially with the mana and Holy Water fueling their bodies. I expect that given your gift, you'll improve faster than they did."

"And how often do I have to do this type of training?" I took a deep breath, expecting bad news. Like, seven days a week or something insane.

"Four times a week," she said. "Three of those are for interval training, and one is a general challenge day based on your progress."

I groaned inwardly. It wasn't as bad as seven days a week. But it was still four times a week of this torture, plus five days a week of running. Ugh. I'd never been the sporty type, as evidenced by my terrible performances today.

But the world needed me, as did my mom. So I was

going to do what I needed to do to pass these trials. Maybe I'd even grow to *like* working out.

Fat chance. I didn't understand how anyone could find this enjoyable. Luckily, I didn't need to enjoy it. I just needed to get good at it.

That was something I could force myself to do. It was going to be grueling and it was going to physically push me more than I'd ever been pushed in my life. But I could do it. I *had* to do it.

"How many weeks is the interval training?" I asked, so I could mentally prepare myself for what I was in for. I was still sitting on the mat on the floor, and after that workout, I didn't intend on getting up until Darra told me to.

"As many weeks as you need to strengthen up to complete the obstacle course."

"What obstacle course?" I looked around, since there was nothing remotely resembling an obstacle course anywhere in the gym.

"Come." Darra smiled slightly and motioned for me to get up. There was a scary twinkle in her eyes—the type that said I was in for another surprise. "I'll show you."

*D*arra led me out of the gym. The sun was now fully up, and I saw movement through the windows of the manor house as the students walked around and got ready for their day.

Hopefully Jessica's first day was getting off to a better start than mine was. The vampire girls better be acting nice to her.

"The obstacle course is on the opposite side of the island," Darra said. "Near where the supernaturals train."

"Why do they train so far away?" I asked. It seemed like it would make more sense to put their training area near the academy.

"Have you ever heard supernaturals train?" She smirked and continued before I could answer. "It can get

187

loud. So we put the training area as far away from the residential area as possible."

"Got it."

"And while supernaturals can run fast, we're not as fast as wyverns and unicorns," she said. "It's why we ride them to get to training—along with the fact that it's therapeutic to have an animal companion."

My chest sparked with joy for the first time since Darra had told me to run on the track. "Do I get to see Annar now?" I asked, although I quickly realized she might not know who Annar was, so I explained, "she's my unicorn from the simulation."

"You do." She smiled. "Just think about her, let her know that you need her, and she'll appear."

I did as instructed. A moment later, two unicorns stood in front of us.

The one closest to Darra was the same one she'd ridden in on yesterday—the spotted gray one with a crystal horn. Next to her was the majestic, white, silver-horned unicorn from my simulation.

Annar.

I squealed her name and ran up to her, throwing my arms around her neck in a hug. She nuzzled into me, happy to see me as well. I definitely understood what Darra meant when she'd said animals were therapeutic. The moment I touched Annar's silky fur, it was like all the stress from the insane workouts I'd just been through melted away.

Once we finished hugging, Annar lowered her head to press the point of her horn gently upon my forehead. "Welcome to Avalon," she spoke into my mind. "I knew we'd be seeing each other again."

"I'm so glad to see you," I said. "This is quite the place, isn't it?"

She didn't have time to respond, because Darra called down to me—she was already seated upon her unicorn.

"You'll be able to spend time with your unicorn later," my trainer said. "But the other students will be heading out for the day soon. I want us to leave before they do."

I looked at Annar's back. In the simulation, I'd only been able to get up there by finding a tall rock to stand on. Trying to jump from the ground had just ended in embarrassment.

After how much I'd embarrassed myself at the track and the gym, I didn't have much to lose. But I still didn't want to give Darra another reason to think me incompetent.

Annar must have sensed my worries, because she lowered herself onto her knees, allowing me to easily climb onto her back.

"Thanks," I said, patting her neck gratefully.

She stood back up, and we were off.

Riding a unicorn across Avalon was incredible. Like in the simulation, I held onto Annar's mane as she ran across the ground. And it wasn't only ground she could run across. Because it turned out unicorns could run across water, too.

I screamed when she headed toward the lake, but Annar's hooves glided across the crystal clear water like magic. Once I realized we weren't going to drown, my screams turned into ones of glee. I would have raised my arms in the air and tried to imitate that scene in *Titanic* when Rose was at the front of the ship and said she was flying, but Annar was running so quickly that I'd surely fall off her back if I tried.

After how pathetic I'd been on the running track and at the gym, there was no need to further embarrass myself by falling off my unicorn and into the lake.

I caught a few glances of Darra running nearby on her unicorn, but I mostly focused on the gorgeous scenery around me. The crystal blue lakes and emerald green mountains were extraordinary. The colors were so strong and bright that I would have thought they were photo shopped if I were looking at a picture instead of seeing them through my own eyes.

We made our way around several more of the mountains before they started leveling out.

On the field ahead, built right over a lake, was the obstacle course. My eyes bulged when I saw it, my grip tightening on Annar's mane. Because it was like those Ninja Warrior courses I'd seen a few times on YouTube. It was *massive*. Seriously huge.

The closer Annar brought me to it, the smaller I felt, until we stopped in front of it and I was staring up at it feeling like an insect.

The course was divided into sections, but each section looked complicated. I was having a difficult time figuring out how a person was supposed to get through it. There were parts where there were ropes, bars, and ladders. But there were other strange things—like a wheel and a nearly vertical wall—that looked impossible to tackle.

To make it worse, bleachers surrounded the course, turning it into an arena of sorts. A coliseum. There were enough seats for the entire population of Avalon.

"You can't be serious," I said to Darra.

"No one ever said the Angel Trials were going to be easy." She smirked and gazed upon the course, her eyes shining in excitement. "You'll be ready to drink from the

Holy Grail once you run the marathon and finish this obstacle course in the allotted time period. And then, you only truly complete the Trials if you drink from the Grail and survive."

Right. Easy peasy.

I wished.

"And even if I survive drinking from the Grail, I still won't be a full Nephilim," I said, recalling what Violet had told me in my orientation.

"Correct." Darra nodded. "You'll need to kill a supernatural to ignite your powers. As Violet explained, that supernatural will be one who has committed grave crimes and has been sentenced to death. He or she will be transported to a satellite island surrounding Avalon. I, another supernatural of your choosing, and the most powerful witch on Avalon will accompany you to that island. We'll make sure you're safe as you hunt down and kill the assigned supernatural so you can come into your powers."

"Why a satellite island?" I asked. "Why not do it on Avalon as well?"

"Since the supernatural in question would be a criminal, he or she wouldn't make it past Arthur's simulation to be allowed onto Avalon," Darra explained. "Therefore, a satellite island must be used. But the satellite island is close enough to Avalon that it's impossible for anyone to get to without already knowing its location. Like Avalon, it's hidden and safe."

"That's good to know," I said, although my mind wasn't truly on our conversation anymore. I was back to staring at the obstacle course, trying to figure out how I'd tackle each section.

"Obviously you can't be expected to complete the course at this point in your training," Darra said. "But would you like to see me demonstrate so you know what you're working toward? I won't use my full vampire strength, so you can see how a human would approach each task."

I could tell by the way she was looking at the course that she didn't *just* want to do it to demonstrate. She wanted to do it for fun.

No matter how hard I trained, I'd *never* find this stuff fun.

"Sure," I said, despite suspecting that seeing her do this would only make it look more intimidating and impossible for me. "Show me how it's done."

# RAVEN

*D*arra jumped off her unicorn and whizzed over to the start of the course. She rubbed her hands together, stared it down with excitement gleaming in her eyes, and set off.

She easily did the beginning—jumping back and forth over big blocks to cross over the water beneath them. The blocks were nearly as far apart as she was tall, but she jumped so gracefully she made it look easy. Next, she held onto a giant log that was wider than her arm-width, letting it take her along a bouncy zip line and landing perfectly on the next platform. She ran across a flat surface that rotated out under her feet, staying just ahead of it to make it to the other side. She swung on a giant swing and took a massive leap to grab onto a rope net, climbing down to the next platform.

She moved between poles that were up to five feet away from each other like a gymnast. She ran toward the nearly vertical wall until she was literally running *up* it and grabbed the top with her hands. From there, she pulled herself up to the top.

With each platform she reached, the obstacle she'd finished completing magically cleaned itself up to return to how it had started.

She did more and more of these stunts, each crazier than the next. Until finally, she reached a chimney shaped obstacle with the front wall cut out. It went thirty feet up in the air. The next platform was at the top of the chimney... except there was no ladder inside.

As if that was going to be a problem for Darra. She jumped into the bottom of the chimney and used her hands and feet to hoist herself up one huge leap at a time, like some kind of supernatural insect. It was insane.

Once she reached the top, she held her arms out in the air and let out a woot of satisfaction. "Done!" she proclaimed, as if that wasn't obvious. "Once you reach this platform, the Earth Angel will be waiting for you with the Grail. You'll drink from it, and will hopefully make supernatural history by being the first human to drink from the Grail and survive."

"Wow." I gazed upon the completed course in amazement—and terror. "I thought you said you were going to tone down your supernatural strength?"

"I *did* tone down my supernatural strength." She leaped off the ridiculously high tower and landed perfectly on her feet in front of me, as if demonstrating what it looked like when she didn't tone down her strength. "This course was designed for humans. Strong, trained humans, but humans nonetheless. So… do you want to have a go?" She motioned to the beginning of the course in challenge.

I looked at her like she was crazy. Because there was zero chance I could complete that course. Even with my gift of determination, my body wasn't strong enough to do what Darra had just done.

But I'd never been one to turn down a challenge.

"You think I have a chance?" I asked.

She snorted and placed her hands on her hips. "I don't think you'll make it through the first obstacle."

"We'll see about that." I jumped off Annar's back, patted her neck for good luck, and jogged over to the beginning of the course.

If I thought it looked intimidating when I was sitting on the back of my unicorn, it looked worse when I was staring straight at it. I was smaller than most of the obstacles. How was I going to manage this?

I clearly wasn't going to manage it right now. Hopefully future me—the one who would be able to run a marathon and would be doing lots of training sessions at the gym—would be able to do it.

But future me wasn't doing this right now. Present me was.

I just needed to take it one obstacle at a time.

The first obstacles were the giant blocks, nearly four feet away from each other. I needed to jump back and forth from each block to reach the opposing platform. There were five blocks, and a sixth one to climb up at the end.

I thought back to how Darra had tackled it. She hadn't hesitated—she'd just run. She'd bounced from one block to another, running on the surface of each one to keep her momentum going.

That was the trick. I couldn't lose momentum. If I did, I'd fall into the water below and fail Darra's challenge to get past the first obstacle.

After my lousy attempt at running and my terrible performance at the gym, I'd had enough of failing for the day. I needed to do what Darra had done. Go for it and don't hesitate. And take *big* jumps. Because the spaces between the blocks were huge.

Not wanting to psych myself out, I took a running start and jumped onto the first block. As planned, I didn't hesitate, using the block to get in two more steps and take the biggest jump possible onto the next block. Surprisingly, I made it and continued onto the next. I *almost* stumbled on the second to last block, but I kept going, not wanting to hold myself back.

The next thing I knew, I was jumping onto the final block and pulling myself up to the platform.

I turned around to look at what I'd just done, breathing heavily. "I did it," I said in wonder, and then I threw my hands up in the air like Darra had after she'd completed the entire course. "Yes!"

I looked over at Darra. She was standing in the bleachers. From the stunned look on her face, she was just as surprised as I was that I'd made it through the first obstacle.

"Wow," she said. "I wasn't expecting that."

Well, if there was one thing I could say about my new trainer, she wasn't afraid to be honest.

"Neither was I," I said, still looking at the completed obstacle in amazement.

"Think you can handle the next part?"

I studied the next obstacle. The giant, log like thing hanging from a zip line. The log was wider than my arms could stretch. At least there were grips to hold onto on the opposite side.

I tried to think about how Darra had approached it. She'd run at it, wrapped her arms and legs around it, and let it slide her down the zip line to drop her off at the next platform.

There was no way this could be harder than the first obstacle.

I ran at it, wrapped my arms and legs around it just like Darra had, held on as tightly as possible, and let it slide me down the track.

The first second or two went well. I could see the next platform coming closer, and I smiled at the fact that I was going to make it.

But there was one part I'd forgotten about when I was watching Darra—the zip line wasn't smooth. Halfway through, it dropped suddenly. I nearly lost my hold around it, but miraculously stopped myself from slipping too far.

Unfortunately, I wasn't able to get a solid enough grip around the log again before the second drop. I flailed off the log and splashed down into the water below.

Under the water, all was silent. A part of myself wanted to stay there, where everything was peaceful and calm, and forget about training and completing the Angel Trials and saving the world.

But I was no quitter. I also couldn't breathe under-water. So I spun myself around to figure out which way was up, swam to the surface, and took a deep breath in.

Darra stood at the side of the obstacle course, holding a big fluffy towel. "Good try," she said, reaching out with her other hand to help me up.

I took it, appreciating the look of respect she gave me as I climbed back onto the land. Especially because I was a sopping mess. Well, my hair and face were sopping messes. My training outfit—along with the parts of my body it touched—were already dry. I assumed it was thanks to some kind of magic.

"Thanks," I said, using the towel to dry off the parts of my body that weren't touching the suit. "I almost had it. If I'd been ready for that stupid drop…" I shook my head and glanced back at the giant log, which had already reverted itself back to the way it had started.

"You'll be ready for it in the actual Trials," she said. "And those are what count."

"So… you believe in me now?" I asked.

"I've believed in you from the first words I heard you speak at the steps of the academy," she said. "Otherwise I wouldn't have volunteered to train you privately."

"Oh," I said, stunned into silence. "Wow. Thanks."

"You're welcome," she said. "But belief doesn't get someone through the Angel Trials. Hard work does. So how about we head back to the gym and continue with your training?"

After this morning, my body was exhausted. I

wanted to go back to my room and collapse into bed. But that wasn't the answer Darra wanted to hear. And if I wanted to train to complete the Angel Trials, going back to bed wasn't an option.

"What are we training next?" I said instead.

Darra beamed. "That's the kind of excitement I like to hear," she said. "Next up is weapon training. This way, if—no *when*—you survive drinking from the Grail, you'll know how to use weapons so you can kill that supernatural and become a Nephilim."

The fact that she truly sounded like she believed I'd survive drinking from the Grail sent a warm burst of confidence through me. Also, weapons were something I wanted to learn to use. I'd seen firsthand how useful they'd been for Noah, Sage, and Thomas on our hunt. I wanted to be able to fight like them, too.

I'd actually already started weapons training a bit with Noah. Hopefully the few moves I'd learned while we'd been on the road would be enough to somewhat impress Darra.

"Cool," I said. "Let's do it."

"What weapon did you choose in Arthur's simulation?" she asked.

"The sword." When I spoke of the magical weapon, I could almost feel it in my hand already. I'd loved using that sword. "Do you have swords like that on Avalon?"

"Like the one from the simulation?" She chuckled. "No. That was a replica of the Holy Sword—more commonly known as Excalibur."

"The one Arthur pulled from the stone?" I widened my eyes, amazed.

"The one and only," she said. "But it's been missing since Arthur's generation of Nephilim. He used it to kill the last demon of their time. No one knows what happened to it afterward."

"Oh." I deflated, disappointed. "That's too bad."

"It is," she agreed, brightening a second later. "But we have lots of swords and knives to train with back at the gym. And it's just your luck that teaching sword and knife fighting is my favorite. So, are you ready to head back?"

"Yes," I said, walking with her back to where our unicorns were nibbling on the grass as they waited for us. "I'm ready."

And surprisingly, despite how grueling this day had been so far, I meant it.

# RAVEN

*I*t turned out I was relatively a natural at sword and knife fighting. At least I had that working in my favor.

Unfortunately, without much strength and endurance training behind me, none of it mattered. Holding a sword for a long period of time was *way* more exhausting than it looked on television shows and movies. As was keeping on my toes to fend off multiple blows.

I supposed that was why Darra wanted me to do all those push-ups and burpees each morning. Ugh.

We used practice weapons instead of the real things so I wouldn't get injured. And even so, I was going to have a *lot* of bruises in the morning. Luckily, Darra said the mana and Holy Water accelerated healing, so I wouldn't be in as much pain as I would have been otherwise.

After getting my butt kicked at the weapons center, we took a short break for lunch. We were once again the only two in the dining hall, since the supernatural students all ate on the other side of the island where they trained.

After lunch, Darra gave me private lessons in weapon strategy and the supernatural world at large. Because if I wanted to fight different supernatural creatures, I had to learn all their strengths and weaknesses so I knew how to beat them. My muscles felt like jelly by that point, so I was more than happy to sit down and learn while the mana and Holy Water I'd had at lunch did its thing to re-energize me. Focusing while so tired was tough, but I managed. Barely.

Finally, once I didn't feel like I was going to fall over just from walking across the room, Darra ended the lesson and declared it was time for HIIT training.

"What's HIIT training?" I asked. It sounded like I was going to be beating someone—or some*thing*—up.

"High intensity interval training," she said.

"Isn't that what we did this morning?"

"That was strength interval training," she said. "This is high intensity."

"Great," I mumbled, following her back out to the track. "Sounds like a blast."

If she noticed my sarcasm, she didn't acknowledge it.

High intensity interval training ended up being just as torturous as it sounded. I had to do thirty seconds of sprinting on the track—full-blown, all out, sprinting. Then thirty seconds of walking. Then sprinting, and then walking, on and on until I collapsed. Literally.

I couldn't breathe. My entire body was drenched in sweat. I stared up at the perfectly clear, blue sky, wondering why I had to be the one to go through torture.

"Great job!" Darra shouted from across the way.

I would have sat up if I had the energy. "Are you kidding?" I said in between tight, wheezing breaths.

She was by my side in an instant. "Lots of students throw up after HIIT training," she said, holding out a bottle of water. "You didn't. So like I said—great job."

The sight of the water encouraged me to sit up. I took it and downed it faster than I've ever downed anything in my life. It was Holy Water—of course—so I felt slightly less like death after drinking it.

"What's next?" I braced myself, expecting the worst.

"The sun's setting soon, so we're done for the day," she said. "Go back inside, take a shower, and come down for dinner at nightfall. Your shifter mate has been pushing to see you, so Prince Jacen has allowed him to dine with us in the evenings."

Noah wasn't my mate yet, but I didn't bother correcting her. I couldn't wait to see him. It hadn't even been twenty-four hours since the last time we saw each other, but it felt like forever.

"I thought Jacen didn't like being called prince?" I asked as we headed back to the manor house.

"He doesn't," she said. "But I've been a vampire for over fifty years, and it's tough to break old habits. Plus, the fact that he doesn't like being a prince doesn't make him less of one."

"Oh," I said, having a sudden realization. "Should I be calling you Princess Darra?"

I'd been addressing her by her first name all day. Hopefully I hadn't been offending her. But she'd introduced herself using only her first name, so I'd assumed that was what she wanted me to call her.

"Darra is fine," she said. "Or Master Darra. Take your pick." From the way she smirked, I could tell she was kidding.

"Good," I said. "I messed up enough on my first day. I'm glad I wasn't addressing you incorrectly on top of everything else."

"You didn't do as badly as you think," she said with a

smile. "Now, go upstairs and shower. Because I promise you don't want to smell the way you do right now when you see your mate at dinner."

# RAVEN

$S$eeing Noah when I entered the dining hall was like a breath of fresh air. He'd grabbed a seat at the end of the long table near the windows, and I ran into his arms the moment I saw him.

Jessica had made some friends while she was training during the day, so I didn't have to worry about looking out for her at dinner. In fact, one of her new "friends" was a very attractive lion shifter around her age. She didn't seem sad to sit with him and his pack instead of with me.

So dinner got to be just Noah and me. I was glad for it—I didn't have the energy for anything else.

"First day was that hard, huh?" Noah asked once I pulled out of the hug.

"You have no idea," I took the seat next to him, since across from him was too far away.

"I have a bit of an idea," he said. "I can feel your exhaustion through the imprint bond."

"Ugh." I buried my face in my hands. "You should have seen everything I have to do. I have to train to run a marathon—a literal marathon. I have to do all these different types of interval trainings. And I have to complete the crazy big obstacle course that looks like it's built for Olympians."

"I saw the course," he said. "It'll be hard. But you'll be able to do it."

I could tell by the easy way he'd said it that he truly believed it.

"Thanks," I said as we helped ourselves to some of the mana in the center of the table. "So, what'd you do today? I'm sure it was better than my awful day."

"Watch this." He smiled, produced a pen from his pocket, and started writing on the napkin at his place setting.

The letters were big and shaky, but when he was done, he'd written his name.

"I know it's not much," he said before I had a chance to say anything. "But my teacher said my progress is impressive in comparison to the other shifters who came here knowing nothing."

"Of course it is," I said. "You're smart. I wouldn't love you if you weren't." I gave my best wink afterward, but it was true. Yes, Noah had been raised in a pack so far removed from society that they didn't know how to read and write. But that certainly didn't make him stupid. "You can't control where you start out in life," I continued. "But you *can* control where you go from there. You're one of the most determined people I know —other that myself, of course." I smiled to show that I was kidding... partly. "You've got this. You'll be reading Shakespeare before you know it."

"Thanks." He glanced down, as if embarrassed. "You have no idea how hard it was to get by in America without knowing how to read and write. It was a good thing I stumbled upon Sage. I would have been lost otherwise..." He trailed off, and we both were silent for a few seconds at the mention of Sage.

God, I was worried for her.

"She's going to be okay," I said, both for Noah's benefit and for mine. "I'm going to complete this grueling training and become a Nephilim. Darra's an amazing trainer—she won't let me fail. And once I'm a Nephilim, then Sage, my mom, and everyone else affected by the demons... they're all going to be okay."

I'd been saying it since arriving on the island. But it

had mostly been for everyone else's benefit, since deep down, I'd doubted myself.

Now I'd survived my first day of training. It had pushed me to limits I hadn't known existed, but I'd done it.

And I finally, truly believed I could be the champion that Avalon—and the entire world—needed.

*I* barely slept for the rest of the day. All I could think about was Kara. Her brother had just died, and I'd been forced to condemn her to a fate as a vampire.

The guilt was eating me away inside. I had to tell her I hadn't sold her out by choice.

As usual, my breakfast glass of blood and shot of complacent potion was delivered by Lavinia after sunset.

"I'd like to go see Kara," I told Lavinia once she'd finished dosing me with the potion. "Azazel said she was also staying in the guest house."

"She is." Lavinia nodded and put the empty needle in a safety container. "But she's being kept safe by Azazel's guards. No vampire is allowed to be in the same room as her. We can't risk any of your kind losing control and feeding on her." She looked at me with disgust, as if she hated what I was.

A part of me couldn't blame her. I hated what I was, too.

But Lavinia was so much worse. Because she was choosing to work with Azazel and help him do whatever his plan was with the gifted humans.

I had no say in the matter.

"I won't harm her," I said. "I just want to talk to her."

"No." Lavinia stuck her nose in the air. "And I don't recommend trying. Unless you want to be confined to your room again."

With that, she strutted out of my room, leaving me alone with the glass of blood.

I drank it down, savoring the delicious taste. Each time I fed, I was both disgusted at myself for drinking blood, and horrified with myself for enjoying it.

Once finished, I could think clearer.

I *wanted* to go to Kara's room to speak with her. But being confined to my room again wouldn't help me long term. Derrick's proposition yesterday made sense. I had the best chance of escaping this place if it was part of a team effort. Therefore, I needed to build trust with the others in the compound. Maybe by doing so, I'd also eventually be allowed to see Kara.

For the first time since being brought to the compound, I put effort into my appearance by doing my hair and putting on actual jeans and a blouse that Lavinia had dropped off when I'd first arrived. Looking in the mirror, it was scary how much I could pass as a human.

How many supernaturals walked secretly amongst us every day with us never knowing the difference? The thought was terrifying.

But I pushed all those worries aside as I left my room. I needed to appear confident and strong for the others at the compound to want to talk to me.

The only other person in the hallway was a demon guarding one of the doors on the other end. Like Azazel, he smelled like burnt wood. I looked him over, and he stared me down with those terrifying red eyes. Like he was warning me not to approach.

He must be the demon guarding Kara's room.

I lowered my head and scurried down the stairs. Now wasn't the time to get in trouble with the demon guards.

The downstairs area was empty. I smelled Lavinia's sickly sweet scent coming from one of the rooms, although the door was closed so I couldn't see what she was doing in there. I walked quickly past that room, heading out of the house and into the center yard.

Unlike mid-afternoon, there were a few people milling about. Most of them sat around in groups, chatting. There was even a young boy playing with action figures on the grass.

All of them distinctly smelled like a forest—like I was standing in the middle of a huge group of evergreen trees. But there was something off about the scent, too. Like it was rotted. Corrupted.

One of them in particular stood out to me. A girl at a small playground off to the side, sitting by herself on one of the swings. She was just sitting there, not swinging, staring out into nothingness ahead of her. She looked so sad and lonely. Like she was falling apart inside, but no one noticed.

But that wasn't what stood out about her the most. Because even from this far away, I could make out her features, thanks to my enhanced vampire vision. And I recognized her.

She was the other girl I'd seen in the Chicago vision with Raven. The dark haired girl who had helped the guys fight off and kill the demon—before Azazel had interfered and stopped that future from happening.

From what I'd seen in that vision, she was on my side. I could only assume she wasn't here of her free will, either.

Most importantly, she might have information about what had happened to Raven.

I started walking toward her. She must have heard me approach, because she looked up, her eyes meeting mine.

Her eyes were red. Demon red. The sight of them stopped me in my tracks.

But her scent... it wasn't that intense burning smell like Azazel and the guard outside Kara's room. She wasn't a demon. Yet she had eyes like them.

Her eyes weren't like that in the vision I'd seen.

What had happened to her between then and now?

I was determined to find out. So I continued my approach, trying as hard as possible to keep at an even pace. I didn't want to rush toward her and scare her away.

Much to my relief, she stayed in the swing. She gripped the chains by her sides and stared up at me. Her long dark hair hung nearly to her waist, her red eyes daring me to speak first. She was definitely the same girl from my vision. But it was clear something in her had broken since then.

"Hi," I said. "Do you mind if I sit?" I motioned to the swing next to hers.

She continued staring, as if sizing me up. "You're Raven's mom," she finally said. Her voice was hollow—

empty. Like she'd made the connection of who I was, but didn't care one way or the other.

My heart leaped at the mention of my daughter, and I plopped myself down onto the swing beside her. "You know Raven?" I asked.

"I did." She nodded. "We traveled together for a while."

I leaned forward, wanting to ask her to tell me everything. But I also remembered why I came out here —to build relationships and trust. And this girl looked so broken that it hurt my heart.

She wasn't going to tell me anything if I didn't gain her trust. I needed to tread carefully.

"What's your name?" I asked, wanting her to be as comfortable talking to me as possible.

"Sage," she answered quickly.

I instantly recognized the name. After Azazel had forced me to tell him my vision, he'd mentioned bringing a Sage back to the Montgomery pack.

He'd clearly succeeded.

"I'm Skylar." I tried to be as bright and cheerful as I could, given the situation. "It's nice to meet you, Sage."

She didn't say the same in return. She just continued giving me that eerie, dead stare. But she apparently didn't mind me sitting there, since she didn't get up and leave. It was like she didn't care what I said or asked, but she wasn't going to make any effort to converse, either.

I worried about her mental state. But I could work with this. After all, I'd raised the most stubborn daughter on the planet. I knew a thing or two about getting angsty young adults to open up and talk.

"So." I smiled, continuing on as if her behavior was completely normal. "How did you meet Raven?"

She blinked a few times, as if trying to remember. "It was the night of her birthday," she finally said. "Azazel needed Raven for something important. He almost was able to get her, but I stopped him. I shouldn't have done it, but I didn't know better at the time." She sounded repentant—as if she'd done something *wrong* by stopping that monster from taking my daughter.

I didn't understand. The Sage from my vision had helped kill that demon in Chicago and she'd been happy about it. What she was saying now didn't line up with what I'd seen.

There was only one logical conclusion. Someone had to be listening to us.

I glanced around, but no one else was near the playground. There were two couples swimming in the pool, cozying up with one another. Another group sat on the patio near the main house, and the boy was still playing with his action figures in the grass. Now that I'd taken note of Sage's eyes, I noticed they all had red eyes, too. And Sage shared their scent—woodsy, with something rotten seeping from the core.

I would have been able to smell if someone else were nearby.

But Sage had been here longer than me. I had to assume she knew what she was doing.

At least she was giving me information. Her view sounded twisted—like she sided with the demons—but it was still information. I needed to work with whatever she was able to tell me.

"I understand," I said, even though I didn't. But the response didn't upset her, which was good. "Do you know why Azazel needed Raven?"

"No," she said, still staring out like a zombie. "His Grace doesn't tell us his grand plan. But whatever he needs the gifted humans for, it will benefit us all. I was foolish by stopping him before. I don't understand why I did it."

"We all do things we don't understand," I said softly, carefully. "I don't blame you for it."

"Neither does Azazel." She gave a small smile, as if this knowledge truly made her feel better. "It was so generous of him to allow me to return to my pack, despite my past actions."

If she was faking it, her performance was startlingly believable.

"This is your pack?" I looked around at the others in the yard—the ones that smelled similar to Sage.

"Yes," she said. "The Montgomery pack. We're the most powerful shifter pack in the state."

"And you allow Azazel to live at your compound?"

"Of course," she said. "We're honored to have His Grace—and his allies—stay with us."

I supposed in this situation, she considered me one of Azazel's "allies."

Maybe that was why she was putting on this act. She thought I was on Azazel's side?

But I wasn't sure. Something about her mannerisms made me feel like she believed what she was saying. So until I had a clearer read on her, I'd continue playing along. And at least she was giving me information. I needed to learn what I could from her about Raven.

"You said you stopped Azazel from taking Raven," I said, bringing the conversation back to what I wanted to know. "What happened next?"

"Raven wasn't my concern, so I let her go." She shrugged. "But at the time, I was helping a friend hunt demons. We were both terribly misguided." She shook her head, as if she was ashamed of her past actions. "Our hunt led us to your apartment. There, we found Raven again. It was after Azazel had taken you, and she was confused."

My poor Raven. She'd been attacked by Azazel, escaped, and returned home—likely in a panic—to find me missing. I couldn't imagine how terrifying that must have been for her.

"What did you do with her from there?" I leaned forward, desperate to know more.

"My hunting partner insisted on bringing her back here."

"*Here?*" I looked around the compound in horror. "To Azazel?"

"His Grace wasn't staying with us yet," Sage said, as if I were silly for not knowing that. "It was before my pack and I allied with him. Noah brought Raven here because he thought he was helping her."

Helping her by bringing her to a compound full of shifters who had sided with Azazel. It didn't make any sense. Sage was clearly giving me a skewed version of the truth.

In my vision, it had looked like Sage and Raven were close. But given what I was hearing from Sage now, it was possible she'd been fooling Raven all along.

I hated Sage for it. But this was the closest I'd come to learning what had happened to Raven since Azazel had taken me from the apartment. Sage's story was twisted, but it was better than nothing.

As long as she was going to talk, I was going to listen.

And so, I asked her more and more questions, learning everything I could about what had happened to my daughter since I'd been taken by Azazel.

## SKYLAR

*I* coaxed Sage to tell me everything, up to when Azazel had taken them in Chicago and dropped Raven off in the bunker.

It wasn't supposed to have happened that way. The four of them—Sage, Noah, Thomas, and Raven—were supposed to have killed that demon and been on their way.

It had only happened that way because Azazel had forced me to share my vision with him.

I wished I were allowed to do readings for myself. Because *something* had happened in that bunker that had allowed Harry, Kara, and Keith to escape. I wanted to know what that something was.

To find out, I either needed to get the complacent potion out of my system so I could do a tarot reading for myself, or speak with Kara. But both of those things were impossible right now. Which meant I needed to continue with the plan Derrick had proposed—building trust with those in the Montgomery compound.

I was just glad Raven had Noah on her side. Sage had told me about the two of them imprinting on one another. The thought of Raven with a shifter was a bit of a shock at first. But I was quickly grateful that someone else out there with power cared about her and was fighting for her.

I couldn't do anything for her in here, so at least she had Noah out there. And from what Sage had said about Noah—that he hadn't "come to his senses and realized Azazel was trying to help them" yet—I assumed Noah was fighting with the good guys.

I also knew from my vision that Noah's eyes weren't red. I'd never seen a shifter other than them and the others at the compound, but my conclusion was that shifters didn't naturally have red eyes.

Something must have happened between then and now that had changed her.

That "something" must have been Azazel.

"So Azazel left Raven in the bunker," I repeated what Sage had told me last. "What happened next?"

"He brought me back home." She smiled serenely, looking around the compound. "He reunited me with my pack. He promised us safety. And we made our alliance official."

"And you're happy about that?" I asked, leaning closer and whispering. "Truly?"

If she'd been pretending this whole time out of fear that I would report anything she said to Azazel, I hoped she might trust me at this point to give me a sign that she needed help.

"Of course I am." She sat back in the swing, as if confused and put off by my question. "Why wouldn't I be?"

"Never mind." I sighed. She clearly didn't trust me yet, or she was too far brainwashed by whatever Azazel had done to her.

The brainwashing must have turned her eyes red. And all the other shifters in the yard had red eyes, too. So there was only one person I could think of who might be able to answer my questions freely.

"Thanks for chatting with me, Sage," I continued, remaining as warm and as friendly as I'd been at the start of our conversation. "Do you happen to know where Derrick might be right now? He's the other vampire who also works for Azazel," I clarified, in case she didn't know him by name.

"You have business with Derrick?" she asked.

"Not business, per se." I glanced down and scuffed

my feet back and forth on the dirt, trying to look embarrassed. The best way to lie was to base it off truth. So I raised my eyes back up to look at her, leaned closer as if telling her a secret, and continued, "His Grace introduced Derrick and I yesterday, and he had Derrick walk me back to my room. The two of us got along nicely. I haven't been able to stop thinking about Derrick since…" I let the sentence hang, allowing Sage to draw her own conclusion.

"Ah." Sage nodded, appearing pleased by my statement. "You want to mate with Derrick. The two of you would make a sensible match."

I couldn't imagine the spunky version of her I'd seen in my vision about Chicago ever referring to a romantic interest as "sensible." But I was just going to go with it. "I think so, too," I said. "So, where do you think I'd find him at this hour?"

"Probably in the library," she said. "Derrick doesn't love the outdoors like us shifters. He prefers having his nose in a book."

"And the library is…"

"In the main house," she said. "If you go in through the back door, you'll make a right. It'll be the second door on the left."

"Thank you, Sage," I said, getting up from the swing.

"It was nice talking with you. I hope we can do it again soon."

"Me too," she said, although from her tone, it didn't sound like she cared one way or the other.

This was definitely *not* the same Sage I'd seen in my vision.

And hopefully, Derrick would know why that was.

*D*errick was in the library, just like Sage had said. He was reclining on an antique sofa, reading a worn leather book. And he was the only person in the room.

"Skylar." He lowered the book onto his lap when I entered. "Nice to run into you again. Were you looking for some new reading material?"

"No." I shut the door behind me, making sure it was completely closed before continuing. "I was looking for you."

He put a bookmark between the pages and closed the book, placing it next to him. "I take it this has to do with our conversation yesterday?"

"I took your advice and started getting to know the others in the compound." I joined him on the sofa, sitting as close as possible given the book between us, and lowered my voice. "I just had a long conversation with Sage. What's wrong with her and all the shifters?"

"You mean the demon bond?" he asked.

"I mean whatever turned their eyes red and is making them blindly follow Azazel."

"The demon bond." He nodded. "That's how greater demons make alliances with shifters. A witch does a spell with dark magic—in this case, that witch was Lavinia—and binds the demon's will to theirs."

"So he's taking away their free will," I said, piecing it together in my mind. "Similar to the way he's using the complacent potion on us."

"It's not similar," he said, his expression grim. "We still have our free will, but the complacent potion prohibits us from acting on it. Once bound to a demon, shifters have no more will of their own. They want what the demon they're bound to wants. Their souls are no longer their own."

"So they're slaves," I said darkly.

"Yes," he said. "I suppose they are."

"So why didn't Azazel blood bind us to him as well?" I asked. "It seems like it would be easier than using the complacent potion."

"Blood binding only works between demons and

shifters," he said, as if it was something everyone should know.

"How come?"

"It's said that shifters originated from demons, similar to how Nephilim originated from angels," he said. "I don't know much beyond that. But from what I've heard, Lavinia's witch circle—the Foster witches—created the spell to form the demon bond thousands of years ago. The knowledge of the spell has been passed down from generation to generation. Now they've allied with Azazel and are binding shifters to him. It's why the Montgomery pack members are being such generous hosts to Azazel and his supporters."

"I see." My stomach twisted with horror at what Azazel had done to Sage and the others. "Can the demon bond be broken?"

"Not that I know of," he said.

"Are you sure?" I couldn't help doubting whose side he was truly on here.

"I'm in the same position that you are." Frustration laced his tone, and he leaned forward so his ice blue eyes were inches away from mine. "We're on the same side. But sitting in here alone together isn't going to help us gain their trust. If anything, it will rouse suspicion that we're plotting against them."

We *were* plotting against them... so I understood his point.

"So what do you suggest we do?" I asked, not backing down. I wasn't easily intimidated, and I wanted to make that clear to him. He might have been a vampire for longer than me, but now that I was a vampire as well, we were the same.

"I suggest we go outside." He stood up and offered his arm to me in the same gentlemanly way he had yesterday. "And that you allow me to introduce you to the rest of the Montgomery pack."

*D*errick and I spent the rest of the night sitting outside, socializing with the demon bound shifters.

Azazel and his demons—other than the one guarding Kara's room—were nowhere to be found. They were apparently off doing business somewhere. The shifters were open with how common it was for Azazel to go out at night. None of them knew what he was doing, but they trusted that whatever it was, it was in their best interest. Especially because like tonight, he often had their alpha—Flint—accompany him to his outings.

Unlike Sage, the other members of the Montgomery pack were able to small talk like normal. The only time I noticed something "off" with them was when Azazel or the demons came up in conversation. Then they turned unemotional, spewing the pro-demon rhetoric that had been put in their minds when Azazel had bound them to him.

Their emotions appeared to be affected by the demon bond as well. They were all cool and levelheaded —to the point where it was eerie. Like their empathy had been stripped from their souls. Even the young boy, Michael, was strangely calm.

I continuously glanced over at Sage on the swing set, worried about her. She was different from the others. More melancholy and sad.

Why was she so different from the rest of her pack?

I'd find out. It would take some digging, but there had to be a reason.

I was listening to a story about how one of their pack members—Linden—had had a fling with a Hollywood A-lister and gotten them all invited to one of her notorious parties on her private island off the coast. It sounded like the type of conversation fraternity guys would have over cans of beer. They were just getting to the point of convincing all the celebrities there to go skinny-dipping with them when someone came out to join us from the main house.

From the intense, smoky smell that filled my nose at their presence, I knew it was a demon.

I turned around, shocked to find a petite, blonde

woman in jeans and a pink tank top standing on the deck. She had the red eyes of a demon, and the scent of a demon, but other than that she looked relatively harmless. Especially because she was holding a device that looked so human—a Kindle.

The shifters silenced in her presence. "Mara," Linden said seriously, the earlier traces of humor gone from his tone. "What can we do for you?"

"I can't get this thing to work." She held up the Kindle, her tone laced with irritation. "I saw the new recruit out here talking to you all, so I thought she might be able to help." She turned her focus to me. "You. Come up to my room and help me."

I shifted uneasily in my seat. It was one thing sitting out here talking to demon bound shifters... but going to the room of a full-blown demon? No, thanks.

"I'm not great with technology," I said. "I'm afraid I won't be much help."

"Don't be ridiculous." Mara placed her free hand on her hip and rolled her eyes. "You were a human like, two weeks ago. Humans are good with technology. You're forced to be, since you don't have the enhanced abilities of supernaturals." She stuck her nose in the air, making her opinion that supernaturals were superior to humans more than clear.

"I'm not sure it works like that..." I trailed. This

demon girl had a serious attitude problem. I would have thought she was a spoiled valley girl if I didn't know otherwise.

Derrick cleared his throat, and I looked to him. "Mara is Azazel's daughter, and she's the chosen mate of the Montgomery alpha," he said, staring at me intensely. "If she wants your assistance, go assist her. Now. It's rude to keep her waiting."

His message was clear. For whatever reason, he wanted me to talk to her.

"All right." I stood up, brushing off dirt from the back of my jeans. "I'll do my best. But I'm really *not* great with technology—so don't say I didn't warn you."

## SKYLAR

*I* followed Mara upstairs and down the hall to her room. It was massive, with a beautiful panoramic view of the Hollywood Hills and the lit-up city down below.

Mara slammed the door shut behind us. Despite the vastness of the room, I felt suddenly trapped. I could also still smell a bit of the woodsy scent of wolf on her. Her demon scent overpowered it, but the smell of wolf was definitely still there.

I would have assumed it was because she was living with wolves. But Derrick lived with wolves as well, and he only smelled like vampire.

Strange.

"So, what's the issue with your Kindle?" I asked, wanting to get this over with as quickly as possible.

"I don't have an issue with my Kindle." She tossed the device onto her bed, where it landed on the pillow. "I've been enjoying reading from it, and find it extremely intuitive to use."

"Okay then..." I trailed, looking from her to the device and then back at her again. The demon girl was up to something. And I had no idea why it involved me. "So why did you ask for my help?"

"I needed to talk to you." She walked over to her bed and perched on the end of it. "You're the only other female here who's not demon bound or who won't go straight to my father with what I'm about to say. But everything we discuss will stay between you and me. Understood?"

I nodded, since I understood, all right.

For reasons unknown to me, Mara wanted confide in me.

This was exactly what Derrick and I had hoped for. Because it was a perfect way to gain her trust.

*If* demons could be trusted. Which I highly doubted. But I was in a tough situation here, and I was open to any possibilities at this point.

Even if it meant playing nice with Azazel's demonic daughter.

"I have a daughter around your age." I smiled, doing my best to make Mara feel comfortable. "Her name's

Raven."

"You and Raven are close?" Mara asked.

"Well, we're very different," I said, since it was true. "But I've always been there for her whenever she needs anything. I'm good at keeping secrets. So whatever's going on, you can tell me. It'll stay between us. I promise."

It was a lie. Azazel could command me to tell him everything I'd discussed with his daughter, and I wouldn't be able to say no, thanks to the complacent potion.

But I'd mention that to her later. *After* she told me her big secret.

"Even given that fact that you're under complacent potion?" She raised a brow, as if she knew she'd cornered me.

"Oh." I frowned, trying to make sure to appear truly distraught and upset at the mention of it. "You're right. With that potion in my system, maybe I wasn't the best person for you to seek out..." I backed toward the door, praying to the Goddess that Mara was desperate enough to talk with me that she'd do it, despite the complacent potion.

"Wait," she said, stopping me in my place. I watched her curiously, and she continued, "My father doesn't notice me enough to think to ask about me. Flint doesn't notice me enough to think to ask about me, even though we're mates. I shouldn't be bothered this much about it, but I am. That's the problem."

Her face crumpled, and she did the last thing I expected—she curled into a ball and started to cry.

*M*y instincts pulled at me to join Mara on the bed to comfort her. So that's what I did.

Out of all the possible things I'd imagined might happen at the Montgomery compound, I never thought I'd be comforting a demon.

"Help me understand," I said to her, and she nodded, clearly wanting to do just that. "You feel ignored by your family and your mate, and you're upset because you're upset about it?"

"Yes." She wiped tears from her eyes, and the redness of them didn't look so intimidating to me anymore. "Demons don't experience emotions—at least not like everyone else does. That's why Earth will be better off with demons in control."

That was up for debate, but I held my tongue, allowing her to continue.

"Ever since the mating ceremony with Flint, I've been different," she said. "I can *feel* things now. I get upset, and angry, and sad, and frustrated. I didn't understand what those feelings were until I started reading." She glanced at the Kindle on the pillow. "But now I think I do. Because all those emotions in the novels I've been reading—that's what I'm feeling, too. It's confusing, and I don't like it. Plus, if my family finds out..." She shook her head, as if that were the most awful thing of all. "They can't find out. They'll think I'm weak. I don't know what they'll do to me if they know what happened to me, but I'm scared to find out."

Everything she said shocked me to the core. I had so many questions, and I wasn't sure where to begin.

But Mara was in a vulnerable spot right now. I had to do everything possible to gain her trust. And firing off question after question wasn't going to do that. "I understand how hard this must be for you," I said, and she sniffed, wiping away another tear. "But you're not alone. Yes, painful emotions are difficult to deal with. But many other emotions—like trust, friendship, kindness, and love—can make you strong."

"Really?" Her eyes were wide and glassy, like a child's. "Because I love Flint, but he doesn't love me anymore. He hasn't loved me since binding himself to my father. It hurts. I don't want to feel pain like this anymore. And my father says you're a prophetess. So I was hoping you could use your gift to figure out how to fix me."

"It's true that I'm a prophetess," I said, and she relaxed a bit at my words, like they gave her hope. "My strongest ability is in reading tarot cards. Unfortunately, your father has commanded that I only do tarot readings for him. Since I'm being given complacent potion, I have no choice but to obey." Her face crumpled, and I continued before she could break down again. "But I know other methods that might help you. Healing crystals, chakra alignment, essential oils, meditation, and various other gifts from nature that can mend the soul. If you're open to those techniques, I can do my best to help you."

There was no way any of those methods were going to strip her emotions from her. They weren't meant to do that. But at the very least, they should help her get her emotions level and under control.

"I'm open to anything at this point." She sat straighter, her eyes slightly brighter. "And if we're doing this, there's one more thing you should know."

"Yes?" I asked, waiting for her to open up and tell me.

She'd certainly had no issue doing that since bringing me to her room.

How long must she have been holding this all inside, desperate for someone to talk to?

She held her hand out, studying it as she shook with fear. Then, right in front of my eyes, her fingers shifted. Into claws.

Wolf claws.

The skin around her hands sprouted fur as well.

She quickly retracted the claws and fur, her hand returning to normal, and stared at me with terrified eyes.

"Have you always been able to do that?" I didn't know much about the abilities of demons, but my guess was no. I only posed the question so she continued to feel comfortable around me.

"It started happening a few days after I mated with Flint." She hung her head, as if ashamed. Then she looked back up at me and continued, "That's the most I've shifted so far. But I know I can do more. I feel the wolf inside of me, aching to be released. I've been controlling her so far by only shifting parts of my body at a time. But it's not enough. I'm terrified I'm going to lose control of my emotions, and she's going to burst out completely, and everyone will see me shift and know I've been tainted."

Well, that explained why she smelled like wolf along with demon.

"How do the others not know?" I asked. "I mean no offense, but you smell slightly of wolf."

"They assume it's because I've mated with Flint—that a part of him rubbed off on me," she said. "They just don't know *how* much rubbed off on me. And they can never find out. Because if they know I'm not pure anymore..." She rubbed her hands over her arms, as if trying to wipe away what she'd become. "Who knows what they'll do to me? There's no one else like this. I'm a freak of nature. I'll never be accepted by anyone ever again."

"That's not true," I said, even though I had no way of knowing if it was true or not. I didn't doubt her that the demons might reject her if they learned about this. But I needed to say *something* to calm her down and make her feel better. "Have you tried talking to Flint about this?" I asked. "I know you said things have been strained between you, but he's your mate. The universe wouldn't have brought you together for no reason."

"You don't understand," she said. "If I tell Flint, he'll go to my father. And he'll take my father's side. That's how the bond works. Flint's will is my father's will. I knew that when I encouraged him to go through with the binding ceremony. I just didn't realize how much it would change him, and how much mating with him would change me…" Her voice wavered at the final part, the tears starting again. She wiped them away, getting control of herself quicker this time. "This is why I need your help. I need you to use your gift to turn me back to what I used to be. Take the wolf away. Take these new feelings away. I don't want any of it."

I watched the girl sadly, knowing full well that what she was asking was beyond anything I could do. At least, it was beyond anything I *knew* I could do.

But Mara was so desperate. So open. It sounded like mating with Flint had somehow humanized her and made her vulnerable. She was the only person living here who had emotions and the freedom to do as she wanted.

If anyone in this compound could be the key to my eventual escape, it was Mara.

The plan formed quickly in my mind. I'd spend time with her, using all the homeopathic remedies I knew to try to "fix" her. Once that didn't work—since those remedies weren't made for something like this—I'd tell her I needed to do tarot readings for her to learn what truly needed to be done to help her. I'd tell her that I could only do tarot readings if she could get me off the complacent potion. Once she did that, I'd tell her we needed to go to holy ground for the spell to work.

When we were far enough away from the compound, I'd run.

In conversation today, the shifters had mentioned a mansion of powerful witches living in Beverly Hills who were actively working against them. The Devereux Circle. I'd find them. If the Devereux witches were truly fighting against the demons—which it sounded like they were—they'd help me.

Mara was looking up at me with so much hope that I felt bad taking advantage of her. But she was a demon. She was the daughter of my enemy.

If I needed to use her to escape and find Raven, then so be it.

"I can help you," I lied, feeling guilty with each word that came out of my mouth. "We'll work together one on one on healing your soul, but it's going to take time. And for your sake, we need to make sure no one else at the compound knows what we're doing."

"That'll be easy," she said. "The shifters here are all afraid to get close to me, since I'm Azazel's daughter and married to their alpha. And my father and Flint are so busy plotting together that they barely pay me any attention. I'll just say I'm bored and you're the best entertainment in this place. They won't think twice about it."

"Perfect," I said. "I'll do what I can with the limited

materials we have here. But it would help if I had more. How much access do you have to the outside world?"

Her eyes hardened—apparently I'd struck a nerve. "After we mated, Flint commanded me not to leave the compound. He said it was for my own protection." The annoyance in her tone got across how she felt about that. "I have free will, so I can technically leave if I wanted to. But the entire pack is making sure I heed Flint's command. So I'm stuck here. But I have access to the internet and Flint's credit cards. Anything I order online appears on the doorstep two days later. It's incredible—like magic."

From the way she was smiling about online delivery, I assumed they didn't have the internet in Hell.

The only hiccup in my plan was that she was stuck here, just like me. But we had time. Surely we could devise a way for her to get around that.

I smiled back at her, hope brewing more and more in my chest. One of the initial commands Azazel had given me under the complacent potion was that I wasn't allowed to communicate with the outside world, including not using the internet. But he never said anything about no one using the internet *for* me. It had probably never crossed his mind that anyone would do that, since everyone at the compound was either a demon devoted to his cause or another supernatural forcefully under his control.

Everyone except for Mara.

"Great," I said. "We can start with a few crystals and essential oils…"

I made a small list for her, and just like that, I was officially working with a demon.

*G*etting myself presentable and putting on a confident appearance at the welcome banquet had taken more energy than anyone knew. I'd managed to put on a good show. But since then, I'd returned to my room, completely depleted.

When I'd become the Earth Angel, no one had warned me about the increased empathy and how it would affect my energy. It wouldn't have changed my decision to drink from the Grail and become an angel, but a warning would have been nice. At least then I would have been able to brace myself and prepare.

I'd always been a relatively energetic person. Even when I was a blood slave in the Vale, I'd been able to keep focused and do what needed to be done to get by each day.

But watching the humans that I'd brought to Avalon die after drinking from the Grail had killed a part of my soul. At least, that's what it felt like.

No spell or potion that the witches and mages had concocted had been able to help me. I'd tried praying to the angels above, asking them for advice about how they dealt with their heightened emotions. But I was only met with radio silence.

Being the only one of my kind on Earth was lonelier than anyone could imagine. And after a time, loneliness hurt. Like a heavy blanket smothering my soul, making it harder to breathe with each passing day.

At least I had Jacen. Without him, I might have given up completely by now.

Jacen was constantly reminding me that I had fire in me, and that becoming a new species was bound to take its toll. He'd experienced something similar when he'd been changed into a vampire and hadn't been able to control his blood lust. It had taken him a year to adjust to his "new normal."

So I held onto that spark buried within myself. No matter how much these new, strong emotions were trying to snuff it out, I refused to let it die.

But for now, we were having dinner in our quarters —just the two of us. Tonight, my mana tasted like grilled cheese and tomato soup. Delicious and comforting.

"I don't want to speak too soon," Jacen said once we'd finished eating. "But I think Raven will finally be the one to drink from the Grail and survive."

"She certainly seems to think she's indestructible." I shrugged, wishing I still had that same faith that Raven seemed to have—the faith that I could do anything. I used to have it. But not anymore.

I glanced out the window to the beautiful mountains outside, remembering how barren they'd been when we'd first arrived. The way the island used to be reflected the way I currently felt. The beauty out there now felt farther away than ever.

"What are you thinking about?" Jacen asked, concerned. He'd been concerned about me since the first human had sipped from the Grail and died.

"The day we first got here," I said, turning back around to look at him. "When I signed the contract, binding myself to Avalon, and we stood in the garden and watched everything bloom back to life." I tried to remember how happy I'd been that day, but I hit a brick wall. Happiness wasn't something I'd been able to feel since condemning so many humans to their deaths. "Everything seemed so full of hope back then. I never imagined we'd be where we are now."

"I know you didn't." Jacen reached across the table and placed his hand over mine, his familiar silver eyes full of love as they gazed deep into my soul. "But Raven's arrival here has renewed my hope. It renewed everyone on Avalon's hope—I saw it at the banquet. Rosella sent her to us for a reason, just like Rosella guided you on the path to becoming the Earth Angel for a reason."

"I do trust Rosella," I said. "I guess I just thought the hardest part would be over after winning the Battle of the Vale."

"None of this will be over until the final demon on Earth is killed for good," he said what I already knew. "But no matter how difficult it gets, I love you, and you love me."

"I do." I nodded. "Of course I love you."

Then he did the last thing I expected.

He slid out of his seat and got down on one knee, gazing up at me with eyes full of endless love. "There's no one else I want by my side while saving the world from demons," he said. "And I'm ready to make our love official before God. So, Annika Pearce, will you do me the honor of becoming my wife?"

He removed a black felt box from his pocket and opened it to reveal a beautiful diamond ring. It was classic and simple—exactly my style.

My eyes lingered on the ring, and then back to Jacen's adoring gaze, filling with tears. "It's beautiful," I said, the words getting stuck in my throat. "But how can we get married when everything here is so grim?"

Honestly, I didn't know how I could get married when my *soul* was so grim.

But I couldn't bring myself to say it. Because I'd yet to feel comfortable voicing how awful I truly felt. I couldn't tell anyone—not even Jacen—how bad my despair was. It was like the world used to be technicolor, but now it was black and white. No matter how hard I tried, I couldn't see the color anymore. Even around the ones I loved the most.

Saying it out loud would make me feel more helpless than I already did.

A wedding day was supposed to be one of the happiest of a person's life. But how could mine be like that when I'd forgotten what happiness felt like?

"This isn't about Avalon, or about the rest of the world," he said, still looking up at me with pure love. "This is about us. We'll overcome every challenge thrown at us, and then some. And we're both immortal, so we should be looking at an eternity together. But if something happens to us—to either of us—I don't want our time here together to end without us being married."

"You mean if we die?" I asked.

"Yes." He nodded, and I was grateful for his honesty,

no matter how dark the circumstances. "I don't know what the Beyond holds, but I want to be married to you before we have to find out. I also think a wedding is *exactly* what Avalon needs to lift everyone's spirits. And most importantly, I love you, and I'll only ever love you. I loved you since the moment I saw you at the Christmas Eve festival at the Vale. So… what do you say? Will you marry me?"

He looked so open and vulnerable that I could barely bring myself to say no.

"Of course I want to marry you," I said, since it was the truth. "But not like this. Not how I feel right now— like there are shadows surrounding me, and I can't see the light, no matter how hard I try. Our wedding day is something that can only happen once, and I want to be able to enjoy it. Anything else isn't fair to either of us."

"You're right." He frowned and started to put the ring away. "It's too soon. I should have realized you weren't ready."

"No." I reached out, stopping him from putting the ring away. "I *do* want to marry you. You're my soul mate, Jacen. My always and forever, for eternity and more. You know that. But we only get to do this once, and I want to do it right. So yes. My answer is yes. But I don't want to feel like *this* on our wedding day." He nodded, and I was glad he understood what I meant, since speaking it out loud again hurt too much to bear. "Once a human is able to drink from the Grail and survive, I think my hope—and my soul—will feel restored, too," I continued. "Then I'll be ready. And if you have as much faith in Raven as you say you do, it doesn't sound like that will be too long from now."

"I do have faith in her." He straightened his shoulders, looking like he truly believed it. "I also have faith that you'll pull through this. Even if we have to wait longer than after the first human survives the Grail, I don't want you feeling anything other than whole and happy on our wedding day. If that means a long engagement, then that's exactly what we'll do."

I smiled, loving how understanding he was about all of this. It wasn't exactly an easy situation.

I was eternally grateful that we'd found each other.

"So… are you going to put that ring on my finger or what?" I asked, glancing at the sparkling diamond.

He removed it from the case, slid it onto my finger, and pulled me into a kiss.

Before I knew what was happening, he swept me off my feet and pulled me onto the bed, and I was staring up into his silver eyes that were more beautiful than any diamond on Earth.

"I love you," I said, smiling up at him through tear-filled eyes as he lowered himself to kiss me again—this time longer, deeper, and full of all the love we felt for each other that was too strong and intense to ever properly speak out loud.

And just then, I felt a flicker within myself... something I almost didn't recognize, since I hadn't felt it in months.

Happiness.

*T*he young boy's body was useless to us after the vampire venom had poisoned him from the inside out. He'd been disposed of immediately after rejecting the change.

Harry, on the other hand... he'd taken to the change well. It had been too easy to find a homeless beggar in LA to throw into the pool house so Harry could drain the human and complete his transition to a vampire.

Azazel had no intention of keeping Harry alive. He'd only kept Skylar because of her unique psychic gift. But we weren't changing gifted humans into vampires to use them for their enhanced abilities.

We were changing them for their blood. The blood of a slain gifted vampire was far more useful to us than their gifts could ever be.

I marched into the pool house, my knife at one side and a stake at the other. I was ready for the fun part.

"It's time?" asked the demon who'd been guarding the door. It was Alex—the demon who was supposed to have been killed by the hunters in Chicago. The one who had kindly allowed Azazel to use his DNA for transformation potion so Azazel could trap and stop the hunters that night instead.

"It's time." I nodded, and we both entered the pool house.

Despite Harry's new vampire scent, it still reeked of wolf inside. Apparently a wolf shifter had been crashing here before Azazel had taken over the compound. And not just any wolf. The legendary First Prophet himself, Noah of the Vale. His stuff was still everywhere, like he thought he was coming back.

From what I'd heard of Noah, he could have been a strong ally for Azazel. But apparently he'd joined the other side.

Pity.

Harry sat serenely on the couch. He'd been given complacent potion and had been ordered to stay where he was, not to speak, and not to fight.

He was helpless.

Just how I liked them.

The bucket I'd requested had already been delivered

to the pool house. It was waiting for us in the kitchen area.

I walked to the table and reached for one of the chairs, turning it around. Then I walked over to the bucket, picked it up, and placed it in front of the chair.

The setup was nearly identical to what we'd been doing in the farmhouse attic above the bunker in Nebraska.

"Prepare the vampire," I ordered Alex.

He swiftly grabbed Harry and stood up in the chair. He held onto Harry's ankles so the new vampire dangled upside-down, his head directly over the bucket. Harry couldn't speak—thank you, complacent potion—but his wide brown eyes spoke of unimaginable confusion and fear. He kept opening his mouth as if trying to say something, but nothing came out.

"Don't worry," I said, drawing the stake from my weapons belt. "This will only hurt for a second."

I sprung forward and drove the stake through his heart.

His eyes unfocused, going blank and still. Dead.

I left the stake where it was. If I removed it, blood would escape from the hole in his chest, and there was no need to make this any messier than necessary. Especially since I was wearing one of my favorite white dresses.

I reached for my dagger next. It was my favored dagger, with a black opal stone at the hilt. The opal had a bit of green gleaming from the inside, making the weapon ebb with power.

There was no time to waste—I didn't want the blood to coagulate. So I sliced the dagger across Harry's neck. Clean and deep.

Crimson blood poured out of the opening, dripping down his face and landing in the bucket. Because he was hanging upside down, it drained quickly. As it drained, I collected a bit of it in a vial to use for my personal potions. Azazel had given me permission to do so, as compensation for everything I was doing for our cause.

Before long, Harry's body was ghostly white, the bucket full of his blood.

I walked over to the bucket and picked it up. "I'm bringing this straight to Her Grace, to make up for the blood we lost when the bunker was raided," I said to Alex, who was still holding onto Harry's ankles. "You know what to do with the body."

The corners of his lips rose in a conspiratorial smile. "Soon He will rise," he said.

"Soon He will rise." I nodded in acknowledgment, and teleported out to deliver the blood to Lilith.

Thank you for reading The Angel Secret! I hope you loved this book as much as I loved writing it. To come chat about the book, hop on over to my Facebook group! CLICK HERE to join.

Get ready for more magic, adventure, and twists in the FINAL book in the series—The Angel Test—on May 30, 2019.

To pre-order The Angel Test on Amazon, CLICK HERE.

To receive an email alert from me when The Angel Test is live on Amazon, CLICK HERE or visit www.michellemadow.com/subscribe and sign up for my newsletter.

To receive a Facebook message from me when The Angel Test is live on Amazon, CLICK HERE or visit manychat.com/L2/michellemadow.

If you haven't read the first season of the Dark World Saga yet—The Vampire Wish—I recommend checking it out while you're waiting for The Angel Test. And the best part is—the series starts with a FREEBIE, The Vampire Rules!

CLICK HERE or visit michellemadow.com/ freevampirerules to grab The Vampire Rules and start reading it now.

To get the freebie, you'll be subscribing to my newsletter. I love connecting with my readers and promise not to spam you. But you're free to unsubscribe at any time.

You can also check out the cover and description for The Vampire Rules below. (You might have to turn the page to see the cover.)

**Before he was a vampire prince, he was just Jacen.**

As one of the most promising athletes in the country, Jacen has his life all mapped out for himself. Train hard, win worldwide swimming championships, and go for the gold in the next Olympics.

But while celebrating a successful swim meet at his hotel bar, he meets a mysterious woman named Laila. Not only is Laila beautiful, but she's smart, witty, and charming. So when she brazenly invites herself up to his room, he jumps at the opportunity to spend the night with her.

He gets far more than he bargained for when she bites his neck and abducts him to the hidden vampire kingdom of the Vale, changing his life forever.

If he can even call it a *life* anymore…

**CLICK HERE or visit michellemadow.com/ freevampirerules to grab The Vampire Rules and start reading now.**

**THE ANGEL SECRET**

Published by Dreamscape Publishing

Copyright © 2019 Michelle Madow

ISBN: 9781090598257

❀ Created with Vellum

19276386R00162

Printed in Great Britain
by Amazon